“You [illegible]d huskily. He reached out, placing his hands on the rock on either side of her.

He was so close Kaylyn could feel the hair on his legs. “Don’t do this,” she whispered, her voice deep in her throat.

“I have to, Kaylyn. And you want me to. You know that, don’t you?”

“I don’t even like you,” she protested.

“You don’t even know me,” he countered, his big hands moving to clasp her shoulders.

“I don’t want to.” She’d passed the protesting stage. Her breathlessness was evidence of her interest, and she knew that King was as caught up in the moment as she. The moonlight made his eyes look silver with desire.

“Your lips want to. They’re pursed, inviting me to do this.”

He reached down and touched her upper lip with his tongue. The shiver that went through her was more than obvious to the man who was invading her mouth, gently at first, then with an intensity that stunned her. Kaylyn’s arms slid around his neck and she felt herself slide snugly against him.

Then it was too late to say no. . . .

WHAT ARE *LOVESWEPT* ROMANCES?

They are stories of true romance and touching emotion. We believe those two very important ingredients are constants in our highly sensual and very believable stories in the *LOVESWEPT* line. Our goal is to give you, the reader, stories of consistently high quality that may sometimes make you laugh, sometimes make you cry, but are always fresh and creative and contain many delightful surprises within their pages.

Most romance fans read an enormous number of books. Those they truly love, they keep. Others may be traded with friends and soon forgotten. We hope that each *LOVESWEPT* romance will be a treasure—a "keeper." We will always try to publish

LOVE STORIES YOU'LL NEVER FORGET
BY AUTHORS YOU'LL ALWAYS REMEMBER

The Editors

LOVESWEPT® • 277

Sandra Chastain

Showdown at Lizard Rock

BANTAM BOOKS
TORONTO • NEW YORK • LONDON • SYDNEY • AUCKLAND

SHOWDOWN AT LIZARD ROCK
A Bantam Book / September 1988

If you would be interested in receiving protective vinyl covers for your Loveswept books, please write to this address for information:

Loveswept
Bantam Books
P.O. Box 985
Hicksville, NY 11802

ISBN 0-553-21923-5

Published simultaneously in the United States and Canada

Bantam Books are published by Bantam Books, a division of Bantam Doubleday Dell Publishing Group, Inc. Its trademark, consisting of the words "Bantam Books" and the portrayal of a rooster, is Registered in U.S. Patent and Trademark Office and in other countries. Marca Registrada. Bantam Books, 666 Fifth Avenue, New York, New York 10103.

PRINTED IN THE UNITED STATES OF AMERICA

O 0 9 8 7 6 5 4 3 2 1

One

"What do you mean, she's naked?" King Vandergriff asked incredulously as he braked his Jeep in a swirl of red Georgia dust. He vaulted to the ground before the motor died and started walking, leaving his construction foreman, Mac Webster, trailing behind.

"Well, she might as well be naked!" Mac exclaimed. "All she's wearing is some kind of see-through robe straight out of Frederick's of Hollywood!"

King strode toward the huge, oddly shaped rock in the distance. A stunned group of construction workers and local residents were gathered around it. Mac caught up with King, fell into step beside him, and pointed at the rock.

"She's up there," he said breathlessly.

King's eyes narrowed with annoyance as he surveyed the scene. Having locals here to gawk at the woman's stunt was bad enough, but even worse was the fact that Vandergriff money was paying construction workers to stand absolutely still, with their eyes glued to the woman atop Lizard Rock. The rock was appropriately named, because it looked just like a giant, slumbering reptile.

"How'd she get up there?" King demanded.

"I don't know. All of a sudden she just appeared out of nowhere and began to climb."

"Damn! They warned me about her." King took his hat off and swatted it impatiently against one muscled thigh. The last thing he needed on this project was some kind of eccentric, do-gooding protestor running around the construction site. He swore under his breath and ran a hand through his hair.

From her spot atop Lizard Rock, Kaylyn Smith watched the two newcomers. The blond giant mauling the tan Stetson had to be King Vandergriff. He was at least a foot taller than his companion, and he moved with the strong, easy stride of a man who knew who he was and where he was going. There was a damn-the-torpedoes, full-speed-ahead look about him.

Good, she thought. She liked men of action, especially when they were overconfident and belligerent. It made knocking them down a notch or two so much more interesting. And from what she'd heard, this man needed knocking down. She intended to win no matter what, but winning was a lot more fun when the opponent was a challenge.

As Luther Peavey back at the nursing home would say, she'd "caught a live one."

"Hey, boss, we got ourselves Spiderwoman!" one worker called to King.

"That's not Spiderwoman," one of the locals corrected him crossly. "That's Katie Smith, the recreation director at the senior citizens' home. And you'd better be careful, or she'll chew you up and spit you out."

"Yeah," another agreed. "She's one tough lady."

"Senior citizens' home?" another worker yelled. "You're kidding! She can't be more than twenty-five!"

"If that's what's waiting for me at the old folks' home," a paunchy driver volunteered from the cab of his bulldozer, "call the ambulance. I'm ready to go."

King ignored the rest of his workers' jokes as he made his way to the rock. While he decided on a course of action he deliberately avoided looking up at the woman who had commandeered the rock. *His* rock, dammit.

Publicity he needed, but not this. He knew who she was. He'd been warned about Kaylyn Smith's opposition to his plans for Lizard Rock and Pretty Springs. He'd also been warned about Kaylyn Smith's incredible beauty.

The body of Wonder Woman, the face of Helen of Troy, and the tenacity of a bulldog. That description of her still echoed in his mind from the previous day at City Hall. Half the city employees—the male half—had spoken of Kaylyn with admiration bordering on worship. The day before that, King had watched men at the county zoning office react with similar sighing devotion when Kaylyn's name was mentioned. All right, so she was some sort of goddess. But what did that fool woman expect to accomplish by taking up residence on his rock?

"She sure is pretty," Mac said.

As they crossed the last few yards King scowled, still refusing to look up at the object of Mac's compliment. "Any half-dressed woman is interesting," he retorted.

"Take a close gander for yourself, boss."

King stopped at the rock's base and squinted upward. His mouth fell open. The men at the county offices had not been wrong. This woman was Cleopatra, Bathsheba, and Lady Godiva rolled into one. Kaylyn Smith had gorgeous legs, golden skin, and an old-world, fragile beauty that would have prompted knights to slay dragons. She wasn't nude, but the hint of what lay beneath the flesh-toned wraparound she wore was more erotic than bare skin ever could have been.

She untied the robe. The crowd gasped, then was silent. Sitting securely on the back of the lizard-shaped rock and staring down at King with determination, she slowly slid her arms out of the revealing garment. As the silk wraparound slithered down, she arranged the long strands of her flaxen hair in a fan across her breasts and back. The wrap pooled around her hips. In her hand was a shiny new steel chain. It trailed across her knees and out of sight down the back side of the rock.

Kaylyn swept the group of men below with a cool gaze. She paused for a triumphant moment before she took the robe in one hand, held it out, and let it fall.

A sharp breeze caught the gauzy fabric and lifted it in the air. Like a flesh-colored parachute, it floated majestically downward, coming to rest like a challenge at King's feet.

"How dramatic," he said sardonically. He ignored both the robe and the goggle-eyed workers as he held out his hands, palms up, in a gesture of supplication. This was going to take some careful diplomacy, he thought. "I'm King Vandergriff," he called up to her. "Will you please come down?"

"Why?" She leaned forward to peer at him over the edge of the rock. A gust of wind swung her hair away from her body.

For a second King felt his chest constrict. The woman was truly magnificent. She wasn't totally nude under all that hair, but the tiny bikini she wore was only a heartbeat away from it.

"Come down," he ordered.

"Why?" she repeated as she smoothed her hair back into place.

"Because I want to talk to you."

"You do?" Her voice held a note of teasing seduction, a lulling invitation to come closer. "You haven't wanted to talk to me for the last three weeks. I've left fourteen messages with your secretary, and you haven't responded to one of them! Pity. A professional conference would have been so much easier on both of us."

The wind tugged devilishly at her hair, tempting his gaze. A shiver raced through him, and it was all he could do to keep his mind on the problem at hand. That was exactly the effect she wanted to have on his concentration, he realized.

"I've been very busy, Ms. Smith," he said in a placating voice.

"So you know my name." Kaylyn hadn't really gotten a good look at her adversary yet. She shifted her position so she could see him without leaning.

"I know your name. Everybody in the county has warned me that you're my sworn enemy. Would you care to explain just why I'm on your hit list?"

"Because you charmed the city council into giving their approval to your plan. You're going to close off the springs and destroy the Lizard—all for the sake of a tennis and golf club with a membership fee so high that none of our locals could afford it if they wanted to. I can't let you do that."

She turned the full force of her disapproval on him, giving him a slow once-over, and almost lost her balance—in more ways than one. She put both hands on Lizard Rock and braced herself. Amazing, she thought. King Vandergriff was amazing.

The mayor had said he was in his mid thirties and was from Texas by way of Denver. Either way he was one of those rare men who looked as if he'd been born to wear a Stetson. His tan boots had been made from some unfortunate reptile, and his red-and-tan plaid shirt couldn't begin to camouflage his firm, muscular chest. This was no urbanite masquerading as a cowboy. He was the real thing.

Back in the heyday of the movie Westerns, King Vandergriff would have been a star in the rugged-idol roles. All he needed was a bandana tied around his neck, a bowie knife, and a horse.

Kaylyn gulped nervously. Lady Godiva hadn't expected a confrontation with John Wayne.

But it wasn't just Vandergriff's awesome physical appearance that made her breath pull short. It was his aura of command and his searing gaze. When he looked up at her in the bright, early-summer sunshine, he didn't even squint.

He was a honey-toned savage in white man's clothing, a smiling, hawk-faced man with hair the color of a palomino. That hair had been casually layered in a style designed to make grown women kill to run their fingers through it.

He looked like the kind of man who lived well and played hard. Kaylyn didn't need a degree in male hormone reaction to realize he hadn't played alone, either. She didn't know how long he and she stared at each other, but when he spoke, she felt as if she were coming out of a deep reverie.

"You arranged this little showdown to get my attention. Well, you have it."

"Good!" she said. "That was the point."

"And what's the point of this little show?"

"If the mountain won't come to Mohammed, Mohammed has to come to the mountain, or, to be more accurate, to the rock." Kaylyn winced a little as she analyzed her analogy, realizing it made no sense.

He smiled drolly. "Well, I hope you're enjoying your little sit-in, because you're welcome to the rock. You aren't getting in anybody's way up there."

"Oh, but I intend to." She held up the chain, nodded at its open padlock, and smiled. "I'm going to snap this lock shut. That ought to hold me until the reporters get here."

"Reporters?" He groaned inwardly. "Tell me you didn't call the media, Ms. Smith."

"Oh, yes. I didn't want anybody to miss out on our little conference. I believe in the sunshine law, you know. The one that says that all official meetings are open to the world."

"That isn't the only thing open to the world," he said wryly. "Aren't you afraid of catching cold?"

"Not at all. I'm very comfortable. What about you? Isn't it a little warm for a hat and a jacket? Or are they a necessary part of the greedy entrepreneur image?"

"Boss," Mac said under his breath, "we'd better get her down before somebody on the highway notices what's going on. Otherwise you'll have the rest of the county here."

King held up a blunt, work-scarred hand and pointed at her. "You're trespassing, Ms. Smith. I am the legal owner of this property now, and if you don't come down peacefully, I'll have you arrested for trespassing."

"I'll bet you would."

"Are you going to come down voluntarily, or do I have to have you hauled off?"

"Oh, I think you're probably going to have to haul me off. At least that's what I'd planned on."

"Fine!"

"And just how do you plan to accomplish that little feat? It will take a bigger man than you to get me down before the reporters get here."

"I think I'm big enough," he said, his voice little more than a growl.

"Big, maybe, but I don't think you have the nerve. You'll never make it up here, not dressed in all those fancy clothes. This rock is as slippery as glass, and hell on fancy boots and jeans. Nope, fancy looks are one thing, but action is another."

"Listen, lady, I've been between a . . . a rock and a hard place more times than you've ever dreamed about. Getting to the top of that rock on my own would be a dead cinch if I wanted to."

"All right, I dare you to equal my feat." She'd counted on forcing him into a response on her terms, but this was working out even better than she'd expected. "I'll give you two minutes. If you can make it up here before the two minutes are up, I won't snap this padlock shut."

King gazed at her in growing anger. Fine, he thought. If she wanted to play rough, then he'd play rougher. Going up and bringing her down himself would probably be the fastest way to handle the problem. He glanced around, spotted a nub of rock, and removed his hat. With great care and nonchalance he placed the hat on the nub. Then he scanned the base of the rock for a foothold.

"Wait just a minute, cowboy," Kaylyn called down. "I said 'equal my feat.' You're wearing too many clothes to begin to do that. What's the matter, are you shy?"

"Never let it be said that King Vandergriff turned down a challenge, Ms. Smith. Start counting." He casually unbuttoned his coat and handed it to Mac, then bent toward him and whispered for nearly half a minute.

Kaylyn watched the foreman nod and smile. Whatever mischief you're planning, it won't work, she told King Vandergriff silently.

He sat down on a smaller rock at the base of the Lizard and pulled his alligator boots off. He tossed his bright red socks after them, then jauntily removed his shirt.

"Taking your time, are you?" she said, taunting him. She craned her head and tried to watch him, but he'd moved so that she could only get a glimpse of brawny, bare chest. Her stomach did a slow freefall into a pit of dread. She hadn't expected him to take up her challenge. She'd just been delaying him, killing time to allow the reporters to get there. Surely he wouldn't come to get her. Surely he wasn't going to take off his clothes. Surely he wasn't going to climb Lizard Rock in plain view of everyone but her.

He was.

"Mr. Vandergriff, I hope you know what you're doing. I'd hate for that nice pair of tailored jeans to get torn." She sat back and forced herself to gaze up at the blue sky with a pretense of unconcern.

"Don't worry, Ms. Smith. My jeans aren't in any danger. I just took them off. I hope you brought along an umbrella or a blanket. I wouldn't want you to get burned up there while we obey the sunshine law—assuming you're not used to nude bathing."

Kaylyn forgot about the sky. She managed a light laugh. "Burned? This isn't the Bahamas, and there're no untanned spots on *my* body."

"Hey, beautiful!" a man called from the crowd of workers below. "When are you going to let us in on the reason for the fight?"

"When the reporters get here," she answered, praying that the distant sound of sirens marked the beginning of the procession she was expecting. She didn't know how long she could keep her solo spot. King Vandergriff was nowhere to be seen, and she assumed he was clinging halfway up the rock. Good.

"I believe I made it within the time limit, didn't I?" he asked in a deep voice, and she jumped in surprise.

King Vandergriff reached the top of the rock and threw his leg across the Lizard's hump so that he was seated beside her.

"Uh, yes." She felt fingers of tension slip along her arms as she glanced down at her watch. "You still have ten seconds to go."

She turned her head warily and gave him a long, leisurely examination, designed to be unnerving. He returned her look with one of his own. He seemed amused and self-satisfied, almost cheerful, but she knew that appearances were deceiving. There was nothing lighthearted about the man sitting beside her.

Nothing ordinary, either.

The outer attire he'd left scattered on the ground below might be conservative, but his briefs were the same flame-red color as his socks. And there was nothing conservative about the way those briefs fit.

He appeared nonchalant about their matching state of undress, but she already knew he was as good at playing one-upmanship as she was. If he thought his actions would intimidate her, he was in for a rude awakening. She quirked her lips. "Hmm . . . believe in color coordination, do you?"

"I try to make certain that everything I do is coordinated, Ms. Smith, darlin'. Nice view you have up here. Now, what was it you said about it taking a 'big' man to get you off this rock? Drop that padlock."

She smiled benignly. She'd done it, she thought. She'd forced him to come to her, and if she wanted the world to know what was happening to Lizard Rock and Pretty Springs, she had her chance.

"I said that I wanted to talk to you," she murmured, her voice deliberately low and teasing. "I had intended our talk to be a bit more private, but you didn't want to cooperate. Cooperation isn't your style."

"Oh, if we're talking style, darlin', I'll admit that you win hands down. Or up—or wherever you want me to put them when I take you off this rock." He gestured toward the padlock. "If you please, Ms.

Smith . . . I won the bet. You're honor-bound not to chain yourself to the rock."

She laughed. "That's right. You did win the bet, didn't you? So I can't chain myself to the rock. Too bad. Ah, well, if you're determined to get me down, have at it. Good luck. You may think that you have wings, but I assure you that you don't."

"Don't need 'em, Ms. Smith."

Without ceremony he knelt beside her and slid one arm under her legs, the other behind her back. She gasped as he lifted her in a single, powerful motion, then stood and turned around. She thought for one breathless second that he was about to jump off the rock.

"What are you doing? You idiot!" She emphasized her last words with an inadvertent jab to his middle.

She barely noticed his "Umph!" as her hand and the chain she was still holding got caught in the golden tresses of her wig and threatened to yank it off. She grabbed King tightly around the neck with one hand and began untangling the chain from her hair. She was pressing herself against his bare chest in a manner so intimate, she felt an unwelcome flush cross her face.

"Careful, darlin'," he whispered rakishly. "Folks are watching."

"Damn! Do be still while I get this chain out of my wig, Mr. Vandergriff. It's rented. Bend your neck forward a little, will you?"

"You're wearing a wig? Thank heavens. With all that hair I was afraid you were half lion."

He shifted her slightly in order to get a better hold. She felt the chain pull across his chest between them. She lifted it over his shoulder and slid her hand across the back of his neck, accidentally rubbing her breasts against him as she moved. Her response to the feel of his chest against her barely covered nipples was instant and powerful. She pulled herself away too quickly, and was taunted by his rich, knowing chuckle.

This man was some old-world savage, she thought, standing triumphantly atop the rock and holding her as the prize. She grimaced. Goodness knows what kind of picture they presented to the onlookers below. For once in her twenty-five years Kaylyn Smith knew that she'd met a man who just might be her match. After a thoughtful moment she smiled with inspiration and batted her eyelashes at him.

"Just promise me that you aren't going to do anything bad to me," she begged in a simpering voice.

Puzzled, King studied her. Suddenly he heard the click of the padlock and felt the pull of the chain around his neck. Her helpless-maiden act had trapped him.

"You've done it now," he said in a lethal tone.

"I have, indeed," she replied happily.

A fire truck and a police car, sirens at full blast, cut across a drainage ditch and stopped alongside the ancient rock.

The chain pulled taut as Kaylyn dropped the padlock against King's bare back. "Dammit, woman!" he muttered, his arms tightening around her.

"You won the bet, cowboy. I didn't chain myself to the rock, but I didn't promise not to chain *you* to the rock. Now, I think we'd better sit down and do some serious talking before those reporters get over here!"

He glared at her, then down at the crowd. "I ought to toss you like a bad apple," he said.

"Oh, no, Brer Fox, please don't throw me in that briar patch," she begged in mock fear.

He glared at her. "Don't try to trick your way out of this. I read Uncle Remus too. You're not Brer Rabbit, and this Brer Fox is no dummy. I know that a lot of those characters down there are your friends. I'm not going to drop you kindly into their arms. If I have to stay up here half naked, so do you." He paused, studying her through squinted eyes. "How about a bet? I bet you this chain and padlock that I can convince everyone that this is a joke."

"It's a deal!" she said. After all, the locals were accustomed to her outrageous acts on behalf of good causes. But they would never approve of an outsider like King Vandergriff sitting on Lizard Rock in nothing but red briefs.

"This is so much fun!" she said happily, and snuggled against him in a manner designed to present a most intriguing photo opportunity for the press. "But I warn you—I'm not Rapunzel and you're not Houdini."

"Stop wiggling around," he ordered. "Who you'd better not be be is Humpty Dumpty." He sat back down on the rock and deposited her beside him with a thump.

"I'll be still," she said sweetly. "Hi, Tom." She waved to Tom Brolin, the editor of the *Pretty Springs Gazette.* Tom had just arrived at the rock with a pack of reporters and photographers. "Tom, meet King Vandergriff."

"What happened to our talk?" King muttered under his breath, his mouth drawn into a fake smile for the reporter's viewing. "Let's talk, you and me—privately."

"Too late," she whispered. "The press is already here." She raised her voice. "Tom, this is His Royal Highness, King Vandergriff. King, this is Tom."

Tom waved. King sighed. "Care to join us topside?" he asked the editor. "The more the merrier." He glared at Kaylyn. "Where is the key to the padlock? I trust it's hidden somewhere on that excuse for a swimsuit."

"Don't be crass, King. Keep on smiling. We're about to have our picture taken."

"Ms. Smith?" a woman called. "This is Iris Raines, TV Nine Evening News." The reporter motioned for the cameraman beside her to begin filming Kaylyn and King. "Would you care to make a statement?"

King groaned. The situation was getting out of hand. . . . No. The situation had gotten out of hand long ago.

A second police care pulled up. Kaylyn watched Darwin Baxter, the district attorney, and the Honorable Homer T. Langley, mayor of Pretty Springs, get out. It looked as if everyone were finally here.

"Why don't we wait for the mayor to get over to the rock?" she suggested, trying to ignore the crackling of the chain and padlock as King fiddled with them. She spoke to him out of one corner of her mouth. "It won't do you any good to try to get away, Mr. Vandergriff. So just relax and look like the mighty Hulk."

"Hulk, hell! If I had a hacksaw, I'd be out of this chain in about ten seconds."

"Poor, trapped dear," she said coyly.

Iris Raines stretched upward, holding a microphone. "Is this protest a political matter?" she asked Kaylyn.

"Oh, this is definitely a political protest," Tom Brolin said, answering for Kaylyn. Tom had been in on her protest plans from the beginning. He was the one who had alerted the news media to her Lady Godiva act at Lizard Rock.

"Make a statement, Katie!" someone urged.

"Her whole body is a statement," one of the construction workers said. "She must be at least six feet tall, and there's not a slack inch on her. Man, have you ever seen such a shape?"

"Ah, she's not nude," a photographer said, disappointed. "She's wearing some kind of bikini under all that hair."

"What's the guy wearin'?" somebody asked.

"Red drawers."

"Nah. Really? Hey, stand up!"

King looked at the gathering crowd with more than a touch of desperation. If he didn't come up with a solution quickly, he was going to be a laughingstock in front of his employees and the county's political leaders. He wasn't worried that Kaylyn Smith's little tactic would bring his construction project to a halt. He was worried that he'd lost his dignity.

"Come one, Kate!" a man yelled cheerfully. "Tell us, who's your captive in the red BVDs?"

"Oh, he's the man who—" she began.

"No, Ms. Smith, do let me," King interjected. "I insist." He turned his best smile on the crowd. "We're so very glad you could come to our ground-breaking ceremony for the Pretty Springs Golf and Tennis Club."

"Hah!" Kaylyn said huffily. She shook her head in disgust at his lie.

"You see," he continued, "I've agreed to save Lizard Rock. My being chained to it is my—my pledge that the rock won't be disturbed by our construction. Once the project is finished, I want you all to come back and tell me what you think of the landscaping."

"All riiight!" one of the photographers yelled.

"In the meantime . . ." King signaled to Mac, who was gaping up at him. "Mac, if you'll just start up the engines on all our equipment, I'd especially like our guests to see our new cherry picker in action before we adjourn to the Waterhole Restaurant for drinks and hors d'oeuvres."

"Now just wait a minute!" Kaylyn said, flinging both feet over the side of the rock. She forgot her plan to keep her modesty and leaned dangerously forward. "I have a few words I'd like to say," she told the crowd. "It isn't only the rock that I'm concerned about. How many of you have ever been swimming in the Pretty Springs?"

"Me!"

"Me too!"

"My whole family comes here, and my mother before me."

One by one most of the voices affirmed their familiarity and affection for the natural springs just beyond the rock.

"Well, that's what this demonstration is all about. Mr. Vandergriff is about to—" But her words were drowned out as King raised his arm and the dirt-moving machines and equipment roared majestically to life.

"He's going to build a private club around the springs!" she screamed over the noise. "And only members will be able to use them!"

"No!" several people yelled in unison.

The reporters close to the rock turned immediately to interview the shocked onlookers who had heard Kaylyn's announcement. Another carload of police pulled in, and uniformed officers began stationing themselves among the crowd.

Kaylyn shouted out her last bit of information. "King Vandergriff's plans call for destroying Pretty Springs!" She turned to King and found him staring at her with a mixture of fury and stunned respect. "King Vandergriff," she yelled, "if you don't shut off those machines, I'm going to see that they run over you!"

"Unlock this chain and I'll turn off the machines. Then you can talk your head off!"

"Word of honor?"

"Word of honor! I've already won the bet, anyway! They believed what I said about this being a planned event!"

Kaylyn looked around at the bulldozers and cherry pickers that surrounded the rock. They were rumbling among the spectators, dispersing them. They crushed beautiful old beds of day lilies and brought her carefully planned demonstration to a halt.

"All right," she said, "but I'm not at all sure you have any honor, and I don't think you convinced anybody!"

She lifted a lock of hair and removed a transparent piece of tape that held a tiny key to her left breast, just above the bikini. "No funny stuff, now," she warned.

"No funny stuff!" he yelled over the sound of the machines.

Kaylyn wished she was surer of the stern-faced blond savage beside her. But short of spending the rest of her life with him atop this rock, she had little choice except to release him. She'd never be able to make herself heard over the noise of his machines, and being heard was the point of the protest. She inserted the key in the padlock and unsnapped it.

King smiled fiendishly. "Now, darlin', we're going down."

"What?"

"Like I said, I like to be prepared. And I'm not Tarzan or The Fly, so I plan ahead."

He swooped her up into his arms once more, stood quickly, and stepped forward into the waiting bucket of the cherry picker. The construction workers burst into spontaneous applause, and the roar of engines began to die.

"You fink! You tricked me!" Kaylyn began to beat on his hairy chest.

"You got it," he said smugly.

The bucket creaked and shimmied under their weight. She closed her eyes and hung on tight, feeling defeated and depressed.

The police chief was waiting by the rock for them. "What's the problem here?" he asked gruffly. "Do you realize that you've got traffic tied up for miles?"

"Arrest her, Chief Newton," King said. "I'd like to charge this woman with trespassing and breaking and entering. I have witnesses." He deposited her into the arms of the startled police officer standing beside the chief.

"Breaking and entering what?" Newton glanced

around the area, then back at King. King suppressed a wince as the chief's disapproving gaze roved over his barely covered body.

"Breaking and entering on my property and defacing my rock," King explained. "She drove a spike into the Lizard's neck."

"I admit I did trespass," Kaylyn said. "But I did not drive a spike into the Lizard. That spike has been there for years."

"You heard her, Chief. She admitted entering the property without permission and refusing to leave when she was requested to do so. I want to press charges."

"You're not serious, are you, Mr. Vandergriff?" Newton asked. "I mean, surely we can work this out."

"Oh, no! I'm dead serious. And I insist that you do your duty. Arrest this woman."

Chief Newton gave Kaylyn a helpless look. "I'm afraid I'll have to take you in, Katie, my girl. What in tarnation did you think you'd accomplish by sitting up on that rock in that garb?"

Kaylyn was fuming silently. Vandergriff wasn't going to have the last say. There was no way she was going to jail. Wait. Unless . . .

"All right, Chief, if that's the case, I'd like to press charges against King Vandergriff for assault with intent to do bodily harm."

"Bull," King retorted. "I didn't do anything to you."

"You grabbed her, son," Newton said. "I saw you. She tried to get away, and you held on. That's intent to do bodily harm in my book. Take them both in, boys, and find them some clothes."

"Oh, dammit! For Pete's sake!" King protested.

His hands were pulled out in front of him, and a pair of handcuffs were snapped on. The police officer carrying Kaylyn deposited her in a patrol car, and the officer leading King opened the door on the opposite side.

"Hey," one of the reporters called out, "what about our refreshments down at the Waterhole?"

King turned to look for Mac. "Mac! Take them to the restaurant and get things rolling. I'll be out of this mess and down there before you're finished."

"Now look what you've done," Kaylyn said to King as two officers slid into the patrol car's front seat. "We're both going to jail. Hey, guys!" She rapped on the divider to get the officers' attention. "Will somebody get over to that van and tell Sandi and Luther what's happening so they can get back to the home?"

"The home? Did I understand you to say 'home'?" King asked.

"Yes, the senior citizens' home. That's where I live."

"Then what I heard was true. I'm dealing with the ultimate do-gooder." He gave a sigh of resignation and leaned back in the seat.

"I live and work in the Pretty Springs Nursing Home. Luther is one of the patients."

"And Sandi? Is that like in Claus?"

"Cool it, King. You're about to push me too far. Hey, Jody," she asked the officer in the passenger seat, "how about a pair of cuffs for Vandergriff's ankles? I think he's a runner."

Jody glanced around. "Cut the jabbering, you two. Katie, where in hell did you find that stripper's outfit?"

"Oh, is that what this is? It came in the last

clothes box sent over to the home. None of our residents could figure out what to do with it. Strippers actually wear this stuff? Can you imagine that?"

The thought of Kaylyn Smith doing a striptease caught King somewhere in the area of his stomach, and lower. He tried to ignore the touch of her bare leg against his, but the sexual tension inside this small, confined area was increasing nonetheless. He wanted desperately to reach the jail so that he could get away from the woman who'd turned his carefully orchestrated world into a circus.

He sensed a sudden mood change in her and knew that she was as aware of the growing tension as he was. She'd shifted her weight so that she could lean against the car door, as far away from him as possible. He considered his alternatives. He'd let them book her. Once she understood that he was serious, he'd drop the charges and let her go. That ought to bring this to an end.

What happened to my damned clothes? he wondered abruptly as the police car turned off the highway and crossed a set of railroad tracks. Those boots had cost him four hundred and fifty dollars, and he didn't want to lose them—not to mention the hat. He definitely didn't want to give up the Stetson. And truthfully, in spite of his bravado, sitting here in his underwear made him feel as foolish as hell.

But still he decided that he could afford to be forgiving. Kaylyn Smith couldn't stop the Pretty Springs project. The land was his, and county officials had approved the project. He'd make a grand gesture. He'd concede that all of this scene today might in some way be his fault. Hell, he'd definitely concede. One way or another, he'd always been able to convince the opposition that he was right. It was his charm.

The car pulled into a parking lot, and Kaylyn stared at the police station. Spending the night in jail wasn't something she was looking forward to, but she was willing if it would help her cause. She rubbed one bare foot against the opposite ankle. She felt an annoying tickle on her anklebone, a tickle that soon turned into a full-fledged, all-out itch. Even her bottom began to burn, and she shifted herself back and forth, trying to relieve some of the torture.

"What's wrong?" King asked sternly, turning to her. "Are you in pain?"

"No, of course not. Something seems to be biting me."

"Let me see."

"No. Stay away."

"Don't be silly. You're breaking out in red splotches." He leaned down and examined her ankles.

"All right, cowboy. Stop ogling my legs."

He was grinning openly when he raised up. "Itching, stinging, little red bumps on your ankles? Does it hurt everywhere else, I hope?"

"Uh . . . no!" she said, trying to still her squirming bottom.

"That's too bad. I think you may have a slight case of poison ivy from your little jaunt through the greenery around Lizard Rock. If you ask the police, I'm sure one of them will be pleased to apply some kind of lotion for you."

"Nonsense, I'll do it myself." She had a sinking suspicion that King was right about the poison ivy.

"Not in jail you won't. Prisoners aren't allowed to have anything that could be fashioned into a weapon.

Sorry, darlin', it looks like you're going to be a little uncomfortable for a few days."

Chief Newton led Kaylyn and King inside, through a tiny office and into a larger room in the back, which held three cells.

"Whoo-eeee, would you look at that," a boozy voice called. "Streakers. The boys at the bar ain't never going to believe this."

Harold Willis, the town drunk, stared blankly at them and Newton. "You can put the lady in here with me, Chief," he volunteered with the grace of someone being presented to the queen. "I'll make sure nobody says nothin' impolite to her."

"Can it, Harold," the chief muttered. He looked at Kaylyn apologetically. "Sorry, Katie, my girl, but you're going to have to share the facilities with Harold and Mr. Vandergriff. Don't think we've ever had a woman in here before. Usually take them over to the county jail. We only have the three cells, and Harold always gets the middle one."

"Fine, just get me something to wear." She walked into the cell next to Harold's and watched the chief lock her door.

"Somebody handed me these clothes to bring along," an officer said. Kaylyn recognized them. They were King's. She glanced over at her adversary. He was being placed in the cell on the other side of Harold. She nodded and smiled.

"Yes, give me the shirt and socks. The rest belong to Mr. Vandergriff. Thanks, Sergeant Williams."

She slipped into King's shirt and put his socks on. She considered for a moment that she should have taken his trousers, too, but there was something too intimate about that idea. She'd manage without.

King Vandergriff really wasn't a savage, she told herself. Savages always ravished their women. King Vandergriff wasn't even royal, unless you could count calling him a royal pain in the . . . No. What the man was, was a renegade, strong and lean and locked in on a purpose. She had to admit that he'd looked as if he belonged on the rock. The more she thought about the day's excitement, the more disturbed she became. She didn't want him to belong.

For every move she'd made, he'd made a countermove. They were probably just about even. She'd failed to change his mind about the springs. She'd failed to convince anyone that his real plans for Lizard Rock and Pretty Springs weren't pretty at all. And she'd ended up in jail.

She had also used the nursing home's van without permission. She'd done that before, but this time she wasn't sure what the director would say about her escapade. And maybe, just maybe, the picture on the front page of the *Pretty Springs Gazette* would be a bit more sensational than she'd planned.

After all, how could she have expected King Vandergriff to strip and join her on the rock? Poor Lizard, he'd probably never live this scandal down. A glance across the cells toward King made her wonder if she could manage to vanquish a man who wore red underwear, cowboy boots, and a Stetson.

If circumstances were different, she might not even want to try.

Two

"Kaylyn, are you all right down there?" King called.

"I'm fine," she lied, trying desperately to keep from scratching the rash that was looking more and more like poison ivy. "No thanks to you," she added in a low voice. "If I could get my hands on you . . ."

"What did you say?" he asked.

A police siren outside drowned out her reply.

"She says she's fine, son," Harold relayed. "She just wants to get her hands on you to thank you."

King peered at Kaylyn through Harold's cell. All he could see of her was a red-and-tan plaid shirt. *His* red-and-tan plaid shirt. When he'd put on his jeans and boots and had seen that he only had his beige jacket, he'd wondered what had happened to his shirt.

"Kaylyn Smith, are you wearing my shirt?"

"Yes, Mr. Vandergriff. Thank you."

"So now you're adding theft to your other charges? I guess I'm going to have to get a restraining order to keep you away from my property."

"I guess you'd better. Because I intend to mess with your property every chance I get."

"What'd I tell you, boy," Harold said, chortling. "She wants to get her hands on your body."

"Come on, Lady Godiva, accept it. There's no way you're going to stop me."

"No? I thought you might have learned something today. It isn't smart to mess with Kaylyn Smith."

"Oh, I don't know. You make your plans and I'll make mine. You like playing games? I know a few I'd like to teach you."

Kaylyn blanched. "We'll see, Mr. Vandergriff. How do you like playing cops and robbers? A little time in jail ought to make my point if my protest didn't. All right, Chief, you can let me out now!"

"No can do, Katie, my girl," the chief called from the front office. "This time it's official and we have to go by the rules. You'll have to wait to be bailed out."

"Oh, my Lord. Now look what you've done, Mr. Vandergriff. I'm due back at the nursing home for a special program tonight. I can't stay in here with a—a pervert. The patients will have a heyday with this little bit of gossip."

"Oh, shucks, you can't leave yet," King said. "This little party is just what I had planned for my day. By the way, what do you do at this nursing home? Teach courses in civil disobedience?"

"It's a combination retirement and nursing home. We offer full care and a place for those who need occasional looking in on. I'm the recreation director."

Kaylyn pulled the voluptuous blond wig off and slung it on the cot. She ran her fingers through her own honey-colored, curly hair while she paced back and forth. King had every right to wonder what kind of recreation director she was, she thought. Everything was getting out of hand. She hadn't intended to let this happen.

Harold stumbled to the side of his cell and peered myopically at her new hair.

"Oh, my goodness," he said, slurring his words. "They've shaved your head. I'm so sorry, ma'am. I didn't know you were going to the Big House. That's the State Pen," he explained to King. "If you two want to be 'together,' I'll trade cells."

"*Harold*," Kaylyn said. "One last time. I don't want any part of Mr. Vandergriff."

"Pity," King said with a drawl. "That might be one thing we could cooperate on, Ms. Smith."

"Too bad." Harold moaned. He turned to King and shook his head slowly. "They've shaved her head," he announced solemnly. "They always do, you know."

"Calm down, Harold," Kaylyn said in exasperation. "I was wearing a wig."

"So you're not bald," King said. "I was beginning to wonder." He leaned against the bars separating the three cells and gazed past Harold at her.

Without the wig she was even more appealing. A cap of damp blond curls curled over her head. Her blue eyes had lost their sparkle and she looked exhausted. Hell, she didn't belong in a jail cell. With a body like that she belonged at some man's breakfast table, flushed and warm from a night of lovemaking.

King turned away. "Damn!" She was doing it to him again, rattling his concentration. Even two cells away, his body was aware of her.

"I wish you'd listen to me," she said sadly. "Why would you want to destroy something for no good reason? That was the whole point of my mission today—to stop the waste and destruction of the springs."

"When you plan a mission, you really do a job on it," he said. "Since you appear to have my undivided attention, tell me more about your protest. You've already made me do more *wasting* today than I can remember."

"They send you to the chair for wasting somebody. I heard it on TV," Harold said.

Kaylyn ignored him. "All right. I'll try to explain." She wished she could get her mind off her itchy ankles and onto her real problem. If she ever got out of this, she'd never, ever, go near poison ivy without a full suit of armor. "The springs, Pretty Springs," she said seriously, "they have to be saved."

"Why, Ms. Smith? I mean, I understand the sentiment you have for the site, but seriously, wouldn't you rather have new money and new jobs in the county?"

She sighed. How could she explain the springs to someone who hadn't seen the results? She'd just end up sounding like some kind of new-age nut. Feeling warm, she unbuttoned the top buttons on the plaid shirt and fanned herself with a torn copy of *People* magazine she'd found on the cell bunk.

"What do you know about the history of the Lizard and the springs?" she asked.

"I know about the springs," Harold said. "I used to swim there."

"I'm afraid I don't know much about either one," King admitted. "They don't look all that special to me. In fact, I tried drinking the water, and it tastes like the ocean when it's dirty."

"That's because you don't have medical problems that respond to the chemicals in the water. If you had ulcers or arthritis, you'd appreciate that 'dirty' salt water."

"You're telling me that the minerals in the water actually heal?" King asked.

"The Cherokees thought so. They brought their old and their sick to drink the water and bathe in it. Of course, I can't give any medical endorsement to the waters; the feds would be down on my head immediately. But even their own inspector admitted that this is the only water like it in America. And I've seen firsthand what it can do."

"Indians, huh? How do you know?"

"That kind of information is passed on. Some of their decendants still take the waters here."

" 'Take the waters'? Hogwash! I'll bet you believe in Ouija boards and the laying on of hands too. Sorry, Kay, I don't buy that kind of hocus-pocus."

"My name is Kaylyn, and I can't say I really expected you to. You know, I tried to buy the site myself."

"You?" He was stunned. "Now we're getting down to it. You want the land. Well, you can forget that. Do you know how long it's taken my brothers and me to come up with investors to back us? You're not about to mess up my land deal."

"Not the land, your highness, only the springs. And just so that you won't be surprised, I haven't given up yet. One way or another, I'm going to protect Pretty Springs."

They heard the sound of voices in the outer office. The door opened.

"Katie? You in there?"

"Tom? Sure. Come on in."

"It's all right, Williams," Tom Brolin assured the sergeant "guarding" them. "I thought she'd want to see me."

Kaylyn was never so glad to see a familiar face. "Oh, Tom, can't you get me out of here?"

"You can't take her away yet," Harold said seriously, reeling as he made his way to the front of his cell. "She hasn't had her last meal."

"What's Harold muttering about?" Tom asked.

"Oh, he saw me take off my wig, and he thought my head had been shaved. He's trying to save me from going to the Big House."

"The Big House?"

"He . . ." King began. "Never mind, it's too complicated to explain."

"I can believe that. Has Kaylyn convinced you to give up your claim to her springs?"

"No way. The springs belong to me. Possession is nine tenths of the law, and I can't allow her to interfere with my project. This Golf and Tennis Club is very important to me."

"Surely you won't destroy them, Vandergriff," Tom said, "once you understand their value."

"Oh, he's not going to destroy them," Kaylyn muttered. "I don't intend to give him a chance." She began to pace back and forth again. "That is, if I can get out of here. I haven't begun to fight."

"No problem," Tom said. But his tone of voice indicated he was cautious. "I've arranged bail. They'll let you out of here in a few minutes."

The door opened again, admitting Mac Webster, King's foreman. "Hello, boss. You about ready to hit the road?"

"I've been ready. Did you post my bond?"

"Not yet. It seems that the judge had a sudden attack of indigestion and took to his bed. But it's in the works."

"Sudden attack of indigestion, my—"

"Now, now, Mr. Vandergriff," Kaylyn said.

"All right, Ms. Smith. Let's just prove your claim. Get the judge, Mac, and drop him in the springs. If the lady is right, he ought to recover instantly."

"So you're beginning to come around to my way of thinking?"

"Only temporarily," King said. "I don't intend to change my plans. And I do know how to fight."

"I'm sure that you probably fight very dirty," Tom said. "Have you had much experience battling with women?"

King gave him a cutting look and said sarcastically, "Why, bite your tongue, Mr. Brolin. I'd never do underhanded things to a lady, at least not without her permission."

He turned to Kaylyn and wished that she'd stop looking do damned martyred. As she stared back at him in exaggerated dismay *he* stared at the top of her creamy breasts in the open vee of her shirt . . . *his* shirt. A bead of perspiration slid into the delicate crease between her breasts. King shut his eyes and shook his head in self-rebuke. *Stop staring at her as if she's ice cream and you're hungry,* he told himself angrily.

"Come on, you two," Tom said, looking back and forth at them. "This isn't getting us anywhere. Why don't we open the cells and let you two kiss and make up?"

"Not on your life," King said. "But I could be persuaded to drop the charges, if she'll do the same. Maybe then we could discuss the situation."

Temporarily shaken by the conciliatory air of the man she had sworn to thwart, Kaylyn could only stare in undisguised disbelief.

Mac held up a bright red terry-cloth robe. "I thought you might need this, boss."

King looked from the robe to Kaylyn and back again. "Maybe we can make a deal, the lady and I."

"What do you want?" she asked.

"First I'll trade you my robe for my shirt." He motioned for Mac to take it to her. "That is, if all the voyeurs present will turn around long enough for you to change."

Tom smiled and covered his eyes. "I'm decent," he said.

"All right, Kay," King directed as Mac held the robe through the cell bars to her. "Put the robe on before you go out. From the sound of things, the party down at the Waterhole must have moved up to the jail."

"Thanks for protecting my image," she said dryly. "Why should I wear this?" She took the robe and looked at it with great distaste. The only thing good about wearing King Vandergriff's brightly colored robe was the possibility that she'd spread her poison ivy to him. Hmmph. He much have a fetish for red clothes.

"Well, I thought that you were through playing show-and-tell for today," he said smoothly.

"Not by the hair of your chinny chin chin," she muttered. She unbuttoned the plaid shirt and dropped it to the floor, then slid her arms into the terry-cloth robe. She tried unsuccessfully to ignore the blatant stare King Vandergriff gave her bikini-clad body before she closed the robe and tied it at the waist.

"Do you have to wear red?" she asked, thoroughly out of sorts.

"Thought you'd understand, woman. I'm kinda partial to red. Never did like anything tame in my colors—or my women. You can return it this evening, darlin'."

Sergeant Williams unlocked Kaylyn's door. "You're out of here, Ms. Smith."

"Good. Give this shirt back to Mr. Vandergriff. I wouldn't want him to get cold during the night."

"What?" King said. "You're not seriously going to leave me in here, are you, Ms. Smith, darlin'?"

"Why, Mr. Vandergriff, I'm afraid you're going to have to wait for the judge to get better. And the only thing that clears up the judge's stomach condition is either a glass of mineral water from Pretty Springs or a good night's sleep. And the springs are off-limits. You said so yourself."

"Wait a minute. Where do you think you're going with my robe? Bring it back here, woman!"

Tom, grinning, held out an arm, and Kaylyn slid her hand through it. "I'm going back to the nursing home to plan my strategy, your highness. You're right. Playtime is definitely over. Nighty night, now!"

The last words Kaylyn Smith heard from the cell behind her were King Vandergriff's furious, colorful cursing, Mac trying to calm him down, and Harold delivering a mournful rendition of "When We Meet on Heaven's Happy Shore."

• • •

"She's what?"

"She's camped out at the springs, complete with tent, cook stove, lounge chairs, and a portable television."

King groaned. "I don't believe it. What are the men doing?"

"They're . . . waiting."

"Mac, you're the job foreman. Couldn't you have prevented this?"

"I should have posted a guard. But it never occurred to me that she'd be back. Sorry, King."

This couldn't be happening to him, King thought. Not only had he spent half the night in jail listening to Harold grieve over Kaylyn's being "sent to the Big House," he hadn't been able to sleep for thinking of her. Now he was facing another day of disruption on the job, disruption that he couldn't afford.

"Reporters?" he asked. "Has she called in the world press this time?"

"I don't think so."

"Then what the hell is she doing?"

"When I left to call you, she was . . . frying sausage."

Twenty minutes later King and Mac were at the construction site. King stopped at the rock and looked up at it with dismay. He wouldn't admit it to anybody, but from the moment he'd put his arms around Kaylyn Smith the day before, he'd felt as if his entire body were racing out of control, leaving his logical calculations in some cottony limbo.

Now this. Even as he stood considering his options, he heard the rich sound of her laughter and knew that he wanted to feel the warmth promised behind those cool blue eyes. But hell, not here, and not on his project. This was business and she was pleasure—pure, muscle-tensing, man-woman pleasure.

"Is she dressed, Mac?"

"She's dressed, but shorts and a tank top don't do much to take the men's minds off what she looks like."

King groaned. She wasn't going to make it easy. But then, when had anything easy been worth having? He straightened his shoulders and strode around Lizard Rock to a cluster of smaller rocks surrounding a large, deep pool of bubbling spring water.

"Good morning, your highness," Kaylyn said sweetly. She poured coffee from a large metal pot into a ceramic cup. "Have some coffee with us." The smell curled around King's nose and wafted in his nostrils as she held out the mug.

"Us" was his construction crew, the entire bunch. Sheepishly the men stood up, mouths paused in mid-chew, holding paper plates filled with half-eaten eggs and pancakes. King surveyed the group angrily.

"Gentlemen, do finish your breakfast. I wouldn't want to be accused of depriving you of your last meals."

The men backed away, and King faced Kaylyn across the springs. She looked like a lithe African lioness ready to defend her territory.

He turned to Mac. "I don't want to see any of the men around this spring again, not as long as she's here."

"Yes, boss."

The mass exodus was complete within seconds, leaving only King and Kaylyn within the circle of rocks around the springs. In the silence he could hear the gurgling of the water as it rose out of the ground and fell over rocks in little waterfalls that ended in the pool.

"You'd better have a cup of coffee," she said. "It's made from spring water. I promise it will calm you down. Grand for the nerves. How did you sleep?"

Kaylyn's plan to remain calm had evaporated the moment she allowed herself to look directly at King Vandergriff. Dammit, she thought, why did he have to resemble Robert Redford and William Hurt rolled into one? He must have a closet full of custom-tailored jeans and Western shirts.

But this morning he was wearing running shoes instead of those alligator boots. He planted his feet apart, and she realized that the confrontation over Pretty Springs was rapidly turning into a personal standoff between the two of them. That wasn't what she wanted. It was the project she was interested in—not the man.

Behind them, machines rumbled into life. King stepped toward her again, then stopped.

"What exactly are you doing, Ms. Smith?" He took another step forward, backing her up against the rock near her cooking table. "Is it me you're challenging?"

"No! I mean, yes. I suppose." His directness caught her off-guard. She swallowed hard and licked her upper lip, staring at his clean-shaven face as if she hadn't spent half the night seeing it in her dreams.

"Fine," he said. "Let's deal with the problem. The springs are mine, and you want them, right?"

"Uh . . . yes. That's about it. I mean, not me, personally. I just want to make certain that they're not destroyed."

She was wearing a bra beneath her tank top, he

noted, but his gaze still kept straying to the rise and fall of her breasts. He could tell that she didn't like his getting too close to her. Cornering her would be a mistake. She didn't give an inch as he glared at her. He'd have to hand it to her. She was tough.

"Ms. Smith . . . Kaylyn, I realize that you think you're doing the right thing, but this isn't going to work. This project is important to me and my company. My brothers and I have worked for a long time to develop it. And even if I wanted to, there is nothing I can do to protect the springs. The Golf and Tennis Club and the retirement community around it will be good for your town. Don't you understand what it means?"

"I do understand, but you can build your project someplace else. Pretty Springs and Lizard Rock have been here for over two hundred thousand years, and there's no way I'm going to let you destroy them."

"You can't stop me, Kaylyn." He was so close to her, he could feel the warmth of her breath on his neck. "The law is on my side."

"Maybe, but as you said yesterday, possession is nine tenths of the law, and right now I'm in possession."

"Why is this place so important to you? Tell the truth."

"I'm human being, King Vandergriff, and I care about all the people who benefit from these waters. Is that so hard for you to understand?"

She was human, all right, he thought. He could see her full breasts heaving in her anger. He wanted to feel her against him, feel her nipples harden and rub against his bare chest as they had the previous day. He wanted to cup her bottom in his hands and pull her tight against his body.

He took a long look at the rocky circle around the springs, then returned his gaze to the woman still holding the coffee cup she'd offered him. He could have her evicted again, end up back on the news, and eventually in court. But sometime in the dawn hours he'd decided that drawing attention to any of her protests would be playing into her hands. No, there had to be another way.

"All right, Kaylyn." He reached out and took the cup from her, then placed it on the folding metal table. "You're obviously trying to get to me. You're in possession of my springs. Fine. You can stay. But there're some rules of occupation."

"Rules?" What was the man up to? she wondered. The way he was looking at her was unsettling. He'd said she could stay. That's what she intended, but there was an intense determination about him, an intenseness she didn't like. "What rules?"

"First you wear more clothes."

"What?"

"It's hard enough for me to keep my men working without this kind of distraction."

"That's your problem, sport. What I wear is my own business. These clothes are perfectly conservative."

"All right, lady, but I think you ought to know that every one of these men is married and has a family. If they lose their jobs because they hang around here gawking at you, you're going to be responsible for some of those human beings you care so much about going hungry."

"Are you sure it's the men you're worried about?" She pursed her lips and hoped like hell that he was as affected by her closeness as she was by his.

He was. She'd gone too far this time. When he

reached out and grazed one of her breasts with his fingers, she gasped and felt her nipple react automatically to his touch.

"Oh, yes," he said, "it's the men I'm worried about. And I'm very much a man, too, Kaylyn Smith, a man who responds to a sensual woman."

He reached out again, and before she was aware of what was happening, she was in his arms and being kissed. For one glorious moment she gave in to the wild renegade who was assaulting her body and her senses. Then she jerked herself free, shoving him back with all her strength.

"Get away from me, you . . . you heathen, and get away from my springs. You're not going to destroy them. I'll stay here till hell freezes over, if that's what it takes to force you to change your mind."

King stepped back, his body protesting, his mind racing with frustration at his inability to focus on the issues. Where the springs were concerned, this woman was absolutely undaunted. He could understand that. His project was as important to him. The law was on his side, and ultimately he would win. But the woman . . . she was another thing entirely. She made him lose control, and that had just stopped being funny.

Yet there was something right about the feel of her in his arms. He'd known that yesterday. They were built for each other. He was six-feet-five, and she must be at least six feet herself. There was nothing petite about her, but she was trim, and he had felt the evidence of physical exercise in the taut muscles of her long legs and slender arms. From the top of her blond hair to her narrow feet, she was a throwback to some Viking princess. And his body was stiffening with the need to have her.

"I'll stay away from you, Ms. Smith," he said. "Enjoy your occupation of the springs. But it won't be long before you're going to see the error of your ways."

"Don't make threats."

"You're welcome to stay. If you intend to camp here, the camping fee is three dollars a night. Or, I'll give you a special weekly rate."

"You're letting me stay, and you're going to charge me to do it? Now just a minute, King Vandergriff. This isn't fun time here. This is serious business." She forgot her fear and stepped closer, intent on making her point. "I insist that you respect my protest and consider my conditions for surrender."

"Ah, darlin', the only surrender I'm interested in discussing with you is a personal one. I think I'm going to have to kiss you again."

"No, please don't. You can't keep kissing me every time I try to state my position. You can't—"

He could and he did, and she decided about halfway into the second kiss that she might need a mediator for these negotiations.

"Is this where I'm supposed to be?"

Kaylyn pulled away, embarrassed by the sound of a familiar voice behind them.

"Dammit, Harold, what are you doing here?" King dropped his arms and took several deep breaths. Trying to conceal the evidence of his need for Kaylyn was nearly impossible.

"You told me to come," Harold said plaintively. "You said you'd give me a job. Remember? Hello, Katie. I'm glad they didn't put you away. Did King break you out too?"

"You got Harold out of jail?" she asked. She was

having a hard time comprehending the town drunk being part of King's work crew.

"It didn't seem fair," King said to her, "to let you go to prison and leave him to grieve alone. Come on, Harold, let's find you something to do to earn your keep. Do you think you can work the coffeepot? We have a supply of *good* water over at the construction trailer."

"Fine," Kaylyn said. "Brew him up a pot, Harold. But I'd use the spring water if I were you. It contains lithium, a very calming mineral. And your new boss badly needs to be calmed down. He's"—she lowered her gaze—"he's a very emotional man."

King smiled. "Don't think your spring water will help, Katie, darlin'. After all, you've been drinking it all along and it hasn't stopped you from getting excited."

"What do you mean?"

"I mean that there are some needs that can't be tranquilized. Sooner or later they erupt into . . . well, you figure it out."

He turned and walked away, leaving Kaylyn wondering whether she'd won or lost their latest battle.

By nightfall she knew that this time even her springs had let her down. Nothing could calm the desire she'd felt when King had kissed her. And throughout the day, in spite of her efforts to control her thoughts, she fantasized several different versions of the eruption he'd predicted. King was the key figure in every one of them.

Three

"Somehow, Katie, I think there must be a better way to do this," Sandi Arnold said. She was unloading placards and signs made by the nursing-home residents. Kaylyn stood beside the van, gathering the protest materials in her arms. The large, deep pool that was Pretty Springs glimmered nearby under the light of a half-moon.

"I wish you'd tell me if there is," Kaylyn said. "I can't give up now, San. I know I'm getting to him." She reached down to scratch the rash on her ankle, realized what she was doing, and stopped herself. The rash reminded her of everything that had happened with King Vandergriff.

Sandi followed her actions with puzzled eyes. "What's that?"

"Poison ivy, from my little trek up the rock."

"Well, it's good to know that you *do* have the same weaknesses as the rest of us mere mortals." Sandi nodded toward the huge blue-and-white travel trailer parked on the far side of the springs. "When did Vandergriff move into the rolling Taj Mahal?"

"Last night." Kaylyn glanced at the magnificent trailer King had set up. It was too close, and it made her uncomfortable. Of course, that was what King had intended. Its presence was a smug, subtle reminder that he was going to provoke her at every turn. "He's hired Harold to be his chief cook and bottle washer. Harold's in heaven. He tells me the trailer is fantastic. It's even air-conditioned."

"Well, I don't know how long you intend on camping out here at the springs," Sandi said, "but there's a cold front heading this way, and that means rain."

Kaylyn looked up at the deceptively clear night sky. "I can deal with that," she said without much enthusiasm.

"Also, before I forget to tell you, you got a call from Tom Brolin, something about a new project for feeding some homeless men. And the Animal Shelter called about a donkey."

Kaylyn sighed. This might be one time when she really was guilty of having too many irons in the fire. Possession might be nine tenths of the law, but none of that mattered if your possession didn't have any effect on the person you were trying to irritate. Sandi was willing to fill in for her at the nursing home for now, but Sandi had her own duties as physical therapist. Sooner or later the occupation of the springs would have to come to an end, whether Kaylyn wanted it to or not. Unless . . .

"Sandi. What did you say about feeding the homeless?"

"I don't know. I'm just passing on Tom's message. He said you'd mentioned trying to put together a kind of soup kitchen for some unemployed people, and he has the food if you can find a place to do it. . . . Now, Katie, what are you thinking? Don't get that look in your eyes."

"Why not? It's perfect, Sandi! You and Tom can load up those men and bring them out here. I'll cook for them, and they'll get a meal and a bath."

"A bath? In that icy water? Yuck! It really is too bad that the water isn't hot."

"I know. I've had the same thought, but it won't matter, because the weather is warm enough. Go through those clothes bags at the home and see what you can find that's usable. We'll distribute food and clean clothes and ask them to walk my picket line in return. That will call attention to both our needs."

"I don't think that's a good idea, Katie. I have the feeling that you're asking for trouble from your landlord."

Kaylyn noted grimly that Sandi, who was usually ready to fall in with any plan Kaylyn concocted, seemed reluctant to cross swords with King Vandergriff. Well, Sandi wouldn't have to. Kaylyn would do it.

"Thanks for bringing out the food, Sandi. Do you think you could man the sit-in spot for a few minutes while I go and phone Tom?"

"Don't leave me here all alone!" Sandi pushed her blond-white hair behind the sweatband around her head and tugged up the sagging waistband of her running pants. "I'm a chickenhearted protestor. I was twenty-nine my last birthday, and I'm getting too old for your escapades."

"So heist yourself a wheelchair from the center. I'll

be right back. My . . . er, neighbor has a phone right in his trailer, and I'm personal friends with his houseboy."

"You mean Harold? I still don't believe that."

"I mean Harold." Kaylyn jumped across the smaller rocks that surrounded the spring and headed for the gleaming trailer. At the door she paused for a moment, then knocked.

"Harold? It's Kaylyn. Are you there?"

The door swung open, and the sound of folk music drifted into the night. "Hello, Ms. Smith. What can I do for you?"

"Harold? Is that you?" Harold had shaved, gotten a haircut, and was wearing a short-sleeved cotton jumpsuit that make him look like a new man.

"Yes, indeedy. What can I do for you?"

"I need to use your phone and to ask you if you'll help Sandi finish unloading the supplies from the van."

"Sure thing!" Harold hurried out to give Sandi a hand.

Kaylyn stepped inside the trailer and gasped. This was no dirty little construction-site trailer. This was a sultan's tent on wheels. Covering the floor was dark red carpet so thick that she felt her feet sink into it. Black leather furniture surrounded a glass-and-ebony coffee table. Beyond a black-and-chrome breakfast bar she could see European red-lacquer cabinets and black-tiled counters.

"It's a bloody bordello," she muttered. "He even has a red phone." She half expected Mae West to come sashaying down the hall any minute.

She called Esther Hainey down at the Animal Shelter and listened as Esther bemoaned the plight of

Matilda, the very pregnant donkey who had been abandoned at the shelter that morning. Kaylyn sighed in distress. She didn't mind providing a foster home for birds, cats, dogs, hamsters, or any of the other small creatures that came to the shelter. But a donkey?

Wait a minute, she thought. She had the *perfect* place. "Esther," Kaylyn said, "can you get somebody to bring her over to Pretty Springs?"

"Why, I guess so. I heard about your little project to save the springs. Are you making any progress?"

"Not yet, but I'm working on it. Send Matilda. King Vandergriff will love having her, I'm sure."

"It's nice of you to set up dates for me," a deep voice said behind Kaylyn. "Who's Matilda?"

Kaylyn turned around quickly. "What are you doing here?" He was standing in the doorway, dusty and disheveled, his hair frosted with red Georgia dust and his face ruddy from working outdoors.

"I live here, remember?"

He sat down on a chair near the door and removed his boots. This time his socks were a soft peach color. Kaylyn tried to concentrate on her phone conversation with Esther. She really did. But thoughts of a pregnant donkey slid out of her mind, replaced with a titillating and unwanted question. Was King Vandergriff's underwear coordinated tonight? It looked for all the world as if she were about to find out. He had removed his shirt and was unzipping his pants.

"What are you doing?" she asked, shocked.

"I'm about to take a bath."

"Right here?"

"Well, not in the kitchen sink. I thought I'd try your springs."

"W-w-well," she said, stuttering like a Victorian matron about to be subjected to a peep show. "Of course. I mean, technically, you do own them. I mean, if you want to bathe in them, that's fine." Dammit! she thought. This was going too far!

"I'm glad you see it that way." He stood and slid the dusty jeans down his hard, muscular legs.

"I do," she whispered. He *was* coordinated. She lifted her gaze from his skimpy peach-colored briefs and saw the knowing amusement on his face.

"Care to slip into your Lady Godiva bikini and join me?" he asked.

"Certainly not. I have to make another phone call. You go on. I'll be here for—for a long time." She said a rattled good-bye to Esther and punched in the number of the *Pretty Springs Gazette.* The phone rang on the other end, and a solemn voice said, "Turner's Mortuary."

"Whoops, wrong number. Sorry."

Blushing, she focused on the phone and tried again.

King chuckled heartily, draped a towel around his waist, then went out the door and slammed it shut behind him with a jaunty slap of his hand. Kaylyn closed her eyes and cursed softly. After two more attempts at calling the newspaper, she heard the words, "*Pretty Springs Gazette,* Tom Brolin speaking."

"Tom. I'm so glad I got you."

"Kaylyn, is there something wrong?"

"Yes! I mean, no. How's my plight impressing the national media?"

"The national press carried you the first day and that's all. Even locally the issue isn't stirring up as much opinion as we'd hoped, though I'm trying. Trouble is, most folks don't share your belief in the medical benefits of the springs, and they'll picnic in their backyards if they can have some of the income King's project promises. Sorry, babe."

She rubbed her forehead wearily. "Well, I've fought tougher battles and won. What about the soup line?"

"The church has volunteered to provide the funds, but they don't have the membership's permission to use the church's facilities yet. Got any ideas?"

"Yes. Bring them here, to the springs. I don't have anything else to do. I'll cook for them for a day or two until we find an answer."

"I think you're running a big risk. King Vandergriff might tolerate *you*, but will he put up with ten or twelve dirty, down-on-their-luck vagrants?"

"He tolerated Harold. As a matter of fact, would you believe that he sprung him and gave him a job here at the site? I couldn't believe it. I think he's actually fond of the old man."

"There may be more to Vandergriff than you've given him credit for. You're sure you want to feed those derelicts?"

"They aren't derelicts, Tom. They're just homeless people like Harold. They don't want handouts, they want work. And I have the perfect answer. If they walk my picket line, I'll pay them off in food and clean clothes."

"Might work, at that. What about a five-o'clock supper? I bring them out about four. We'll get them cleaned up and fed, and they'll have a few minutes before dark to walk your picket line near the road. They don't have to picket long to make your point."

"Fine. You bring the food in the morning."

Kaylyn hung up the phone and glanced out the window. She gasped. From where she was standing, she could see straight into her camp area. Now she understood why King had placed his trailer in this spot. He could watch every move she made, including . . . damn! He could see her bathing spot. Had he been watching her as she took her morning bath and her afternoon swim?

At that moment King came into view. He stood majestically at the edge of the springs, wearing nothing but his briefs. He walked gracefully into the water, stood for a moment in the moonlight, then bent forward and dived out of sight. When he surfaced, he shook his head, slinging water from his thick golden hair.

Where were Harold and Sandi? Kaylyn wondered abruptly. She couldn't see either of them, and the van was gone. She watched King slide both hands up and down his chest. He shrugged his powerful shoulders to fling some of the water from them, then waded toward the edge of the pool. He stopped in knee-deep water and turned slightly so that she could see his . . . Well, she could see that his underwear was as revealing as her bikini had been three days ago.

She suddenly realized that he was looking straight at her. He smiled broadly and moved his head in a come-hither nod.

That turkey, she thought. He knew she was watching him! And he was posing just for her benefit! He also knew *what*, specifically, she was watching. She was certain he suspected that her heart was pounding against her chest wall and that an exquisite warmth was centered low in her stomach.

He was the most supremely self-confident man she'd ever encountered. And possibly the most appealing.

Well, he was in for a big surprise. He'd invited her to accompany him in a swim. That was just what she'd do. She still had the string bikini, and what was good for the gander—the king gander—was good for the goose. Or something like that. It was hard to keep her thoughts straight under the circumstances.

She went outside and strode across the rocky border dividing their camps. King bowed at her as she passed. Inside her tent, she changed into her bikini. When she returned, he was stretched out on a flat, moonlit rock adjacent to the pool, his eyes closed. She heard his exaggerated sigh.

"You know, darlin'," he murmured, "you're right about one thing."

"Oh? What's that?"

"These springs are very refreshing. I can see why you like to swim in them."

"Too bad you don't have some kind of medical condition so that I could prove my theory." She was standing over him as she answered.

He opened his eyes and saw the incredible sight of Kaylyn Smith in the bikini again. Damn. This time no wig provided a shield between her appealing body and his reaction. He'd been more than half aroused *before* he'd bathed in the springs, and now his own scanty attire left him no secrets. He watched her gaze flicker over him quickly, pause, then move away.

"Awwwk!" He rolled off the rock into the water,

grasping his chest in exaggerated pain. "I think I'm having an attack of the vapors! Save me."

She laughed and plunged into the opposite end of the pool. "Wrong kind of problem, your highness. Though the springs have been known to lower a man's blood pressure, I don't think they'll have an effect on *your* predicament." She hesitated and her voice became sly. "There was a time in the early 1900s when it was believed that the springs helped treat impotence."

"Lady, that is a problem I definitely don't have, in spite of the temperature of this water. Doesn't it ever get warm?"

"Well, warmer maybe, in the middle of the day. But this water comes from the ice age, when it was trapped down in the underlying rock strata. It's been there ever since. That's what makes the mineral content so high—the water leaches minerals from the rocks. There aren't any other springs with this composition, except one in the Caribbean."

"I vote for the Caribbean." He stood up, the water lapping just below his nipples. Even in the shadows she could tell that his gaze was on her.

She paddled to a deep spot and treaded water slowly. She was grateful for the man's undivided attention. That was what she'd wanted. Now that she had it, she wasn't going to waste it. She began to speak softly, carefully.

King listened to Kaylyn's impassioned defense of the springs, but his attention wasn't on the information. It was on the woman giving it. He'd never met anybody so dedicated. He'd never seen a woman so natural and open about her emotions. He shook his head. He'd also never passed up an opportunity to romance a fascinating woman, troublesome or not. Why start now?

He dived suddenly, cut through the water in front of her like a sleek dolphin, and surfaced inches from her face. "Tell me more," he whispered.

She started back, dog-paddling. "Yes, well, we know that the interest in these springs dates back to the time of the Cherokees. They recognized its healing properties. They even held religious ceremonies on Lizard Rock. And as I keep trying to explain to you, the interest continued into the 1900s."

He treaded water, listening intently, keeping close to her as she talked. "So explain to me, darlin'."

"The water was bottled and sold for all kinds of medicinal purposes. There was even a resort hotel here, where people came to take the baths." She reached the rock on the opposite side of the pool, a shallower spot where she could stand with the water just below her collarbones. He followed her.

"How nice," he said huskily. "History repeating itself. Now I'm going to build a resort here. You're beautiful, Kaylyn Smith." He reached out and placed his hands on the rock on either side of her.

He was so close, she could feel the hair on his legs. Her nipples grazed his chest, and her lower body recognized and responded to the contact it made with his.

"Don't do this," she whispered, her voice deep and husky.

"I have to, Kaylyn. And you want me to. You know that, don't you?"

"I don't even like you," she said.

"You don't know me," he corrected her, his big hands moving to clasp her shoulders.

"I don't want to." She'd passed the protesting stage. Her breathlessness was evidence of her interest, and she knew that King was as caught up in the moment as she. The moonlight made his eyes look silver with desire.

"Your lips want to," he whispered. "They're pursed, inviting me to do this."

He bent down and touched her upper lip with his tongue. The shiver that ricocheted through her was more than obvious to the man now invading her mouth, gently at first, then with an intensity that stunned her. Her arms slid around his neck, and she felt herself slide tightly against him. He pulled her legs around his hips.

"Kaylyn, I . . ."

"King, I . . ."

"Hello! Kaylyn? Are you here?" The woman's voice trilled across the springs and jerked both Kaylyn and King back to reality.

"Damn!" he swore. He gently guided Kaylyn to the shallow side. "Now what?"

As if in answer, a raucous, earsplitting bray pierced the silence.

"What the hell?" He pulled himself out of the springs and wrapped his towel around his lower body. Kaylyn followed suit, slipping her arms into an oversize shirt hanging on a nearby bush. She turned the switch on her battery-powered lantern, and a bright pool of light illuminated the area.

"We're here," the unseen woman said. "We came right away. It's a good thing the shelter is so close by." An odd-shaped little woman wearing army khakis and an Australian bush hat walked into the clearing leading a very round, very reluctant brown donkey. The donkey took one look at King, yanked its lead rope out of the woman's hands, and trotted forward to rub its head against King's arm.

The woman laughed. "This is Matilda. I'm so glad you two have agreed to give her a foster home. She's due to foal any day now."

King suddenly noticed the stack of placards and protest signs piled beside Kaylyn's tent. "What are those?" he asked.

"For my picket line."

"What's this donkey doing here?"

"I'm giving her a foster home, King."

She felt a twinge of guilt at his stunned expression. Maybe she'd gone too far. Maybe she should have given him an opportunity to talk before—

"Foster home?" he repeated angrily. "For a pregnant donkey? That does it!" He whirled and stomped back toward his trailer. Matilda trotted after him, braying in protest at being left behind. Kaylyn ran after them both.

"Get that animal away from me!" King stood on the top step of his travel trailer and glared at Kaylyn.

"I think she likes you." Kaylyn grabbed the trailing end of Matilda's rope and braced her feet. She threw a hopeful glance over her shoulder at Esther, who was spellbound by the sight of King Vandergriff wearing a skimpy black towel tied loosely about his hips.

"Esther? Esther!" Kaylyn called to no avail. "Esther, did you see Sandi and Harold?"

"Um . . . yes. They're over by Lizard Rock talking to a man named Mac."

Matilda lunged and planted her front hooves on the trailer's middle step.

"Kaylyn!" King warned.

This was one time Kaylyn couldn't blame King for his fury. She had to have help, and it was obvious that Esther wasn't going to be it. "Sandi!" she yelled desperately. "Sandi, come and help me!"

"I'm on the way!" a voice called. "Harold and I just went down to mark the entranceway for the soup line. Good heavens!"

Sandi and Harold ran up to the trailer. Mac Webster followed them. "What are you doing, boss?" Mac asked. He glanced from Kaylyn to Matilda to King. "Are we playing show-and-tell again?"

"If you two traitors have a moment," King said tightly, glaring at Harold and Mac, "I'd appreciate it if you'd get this miniature mule away from this door and off my property. *Now!*"

"Over my dead body," Kaylyn said.

He shoved Matilda back and jerked open the trailer door. "That, my darlin' Ms. Smith, might very well be arranged." He stepped inside and slammed the door behind him.

Two things amazed Kaylyn. Matilda allowed herself to be tethered quietly in a patch of greenery just behind the tent, and Harold reported to her for kitchen duty as soon as King left his trailer the next morning.

"Aren't you worried about your job if you help me cook soup for the homeless?" she asked.

"Nope. King talks tough, but he'd got a soft spot under all that hard blarney. Did you know that he had a worthless daddy?"

"No. I don't know much about King."

"A gambler. Started drinking, lost everything, just like me. Died—bad. I don't wanna die bad. Think that's why King took me in?"

Kaylyn stared at the ground, thinking. King was a mystery man. He was head of his own development company, wealthy, and heart-stoppingly gorgeous—plenty of reasons for him to treat the rest of the world with nonchalant unconcern. And yet he had taken Harold home and given him a job. Matilda adored him, and Kaylyn had decided long ago that animals were good at sizing a person up.

"Where does King's family live, Harold?" she asked.

"All over. One brother is an architect in Texas, and the other is overseeing a construction project in Arizona. He has a sister somewhere. King moves around from one place to another. Lives in that trailer, he does."

Kaylyn frowned thoughtfully. Maybe King Vandergriff had never had a real home. Maybe he'd never settled down in one spot long enough to feel a sense of commitment to the community. He couldn't appreciate her sentiment over Pretty Springs because he'd never felt sentiment for a place.

No, she was filling in blanks with her own observations. What she needed were facts, not suppositions. Just because every time she said his name she felt a rush of warmth inside was no reason to feel sympathy for her enemy.

By the time late afternoon rolled around, every man on King's payroll had concocted some excuse to check out the delicious aromas wafting through the air over the construction site. Kaylyn told them when supper was and invited them to join in. King's day-long absence only added anticipation to the coming events.

At four Kaylyn changed from her working costume of cutoffs and an oversize T-shirt to a pink cotton sundress and flat white sandals. She sorted out the clothing Sandi had brought and arranged her soup bowls and iced-tea glasses for easy access.

By five o'clock, nine men—some of the them winos, some of them just plain down-on-their-luck drifters—had bathed in the pool and were sitting around the circle eating soup. By six o'clock, seven workers from the construction site had joined the crowd. A lively conversation sprang up between the mismatched groups, and Kaylyn quickly saw that something unexpected was happening. Following King's lead in rescuing and bringing Harold home, the workers were sounding out the homeless to determine what could be done to help them.

After dinner the homeless men cheerfully hoisted Kaylyn's picket signs and formed a procession at the entrance to the construction site. The picketing was uneventful, and after thirty minutes the men were given rides back into town by the departing workmen.

By seven o'clock, Kaylyn and Harold had the camp shipshape, and Matilda bedded down for the night. By eight-thirty, King returned from wherever he'd been. He went straight to his trailer without speaking to Kaylyn. She sat outside her tent, watching for glimpses of him as he walked back and forth behind the trailer's windows.

Windows with nice bug-proof screens, she thought enviously. She was swatting mosquitoes madly, wishing for a can of repellent. By nine o'clock, clouds covered the night sky. Rain began to fall. She hurried inside her tent.

The tent had been more or less waterproofed the last time she'd used it. But three years of creases had put several glitches in the fabric, and in no time she was shivering and wet. She stared through the tent flaps at King's snug trailer and kept telling herself that her suffering was worthwhile. Sandi had taken the van back to the home, so Kaylyn couldn't leave even if she wanted to. It was too far to walk, and the only phone close by belonged to King Vandergriff.

Matilda began to announce her displeasure with the rain.

"Sorry, old girl," Kaylyn yelled to her. "This tent isn't big enough for you and me, and I don't think you'd like it that much if it was."

Poor, pregnant Matilda had no shelter, she thought, and considered the possibilities. There wasn't any shelter on the construction site, except for the pan of one of the big bulldozers. Maybe she could anchor Matilda beneath the huge shovel.

Gritting her teeth, she lifted the flap on her tent and stepped out into the downpour. She untied Matilda and began leading her around the back side of the rocks to where the heavy equipment was parked. But Matilda had a mind of her own. Before Kaylyn could stop her, she jerked away and darted toward King's trailer. She halted beneath the porch-sized awning attached to one side of the trailer.

"Oh, no!" Kaylyn cried. She ran to the donkey and tugged at her lead rope. "Matilda, *please* come with me. Things are bad enough without you making everything worse. I don't care if you *are* an expectant mother, you're about to get me killed."

Matilda brayed. Matilda stayed.

King slung his door open. "What the hell?" He stared in disbelief at the sight of a soaking wet Kaylyn trying diligently to pull the stubborn donkey from under his awning.

Kaylyn stared back at him. The robe he was wearing tonight was black. It was satin, and it was dry.

"I'm sorry, King, but Matilda doesn't like summer rainstorms. I can't seem to budge her."

"Try offering her a nice hot bowl of soup. Maybe that will entice her over to your campsite," he said sarcastically. "It enticed everybody else."

"Not you."

"I didn't think you'd have enough for one more guest, what with all those other men. Besides, I wasn't invited."

She started to reply, then recalled her earlier conversation with Harold. King had known she was feeding the homeless men, yet he hadn't interfered. He had known that his own workers had joined in, yet he hadn't threatened to fire any of them. He hadn't called the police to break up her picket lines.

"I have some some soup left," she said. "I'll trade you a bowl for a dry spot to wait out the shower."

"Just you and the donkey?" His suspicion was obvious.

"Who else do you see standing out here?"

"Who knows how many others might be hiding behind the rocks, ready to jump out and invade my trailer?"

"Everybody else is back on their own respective turf, minding their own business. Where's Harold?"

"Harold may work here, but he doesn't sleep here. He prefers his regular cell down at the jail."

"You're kidding."

"Nope. You may get Harold out of the jail, but you'll never get the jail out of Harold." King sighed with defeat. "Leave the damned donkey and come inside."

"Just a minute." She dropped Matilda's rope and dashed back to the canvas lean-to she'd fashioned to cover her supplies. She found her flashlight and pointed it toward the pool until she located a rope hanging from a tree. The rope was tied around a quart jar of soup that she'd submerged in the cold spring water. She pulled the jar up and splashed back to the trailer.

"You can come in, Kaylyn," King said, "but I don't want you dripping all over my carpet. Leave the dress outside." He held up another of his apparently large collection of robes, this one of red-and-black velour. It looked invitingly warm.

"Close you eyes," she instructed, placing the jar just inside the door.

"After you showed off in that skimpy outfit on the rock and in the pool, you're turning modest on me?" He chuckled. She obviously hadn't realized that the wet dress was hugging her body in a way that made modesty a lost cause. "Oh, all right."

He turned his head dramatically, exaggerating a gallant attitude. Out of the corner of one eye he watched her shimmy her dress down and off. She wore nothing but panties, and her breasts gleamed with rainwater. She slid her arms into his robe, then hugged its warmth around her.

Matilda gave a short, soft bray of good-bye as Kaylyn

stepped inside the trailer. King looked out, winked at the donkey, then closed the door.

"Sit down," he said to Kaylyn. "And put these on your feet." He handed her a pair of his slippers, and she stifled an urge to gape at them. They looked like large, fuzzy black-and-red teddy bears.

"What do they do, cuddle up and play footsie?" she asked drolly.

"No, they're called Huggies," he said defensively. "A friend of mine makes stuffed dolls and clowns. As a joke, she turned one of her doll designs into slippers for me."

"So you're a teddy-bear sort of guy."

His voice held wry warning. "*She* chose the bears for me. She said they were the most lovable of her designs, and that I was in need of something to love."

"And are you?"

"No comment."

"Hmm." Kaylyn realized that the bear slippers had a used look about them, and she nearly laughed out loud at the idea of King Vandergriff padding around his luxury trailer in them. The notion was unsettling. The kind of man who would put on silly-looking shoes like these must be very secure in his masculinity. He must also have a whimsical, gentle outlook on life.

"Your friend has odd talents," she said distractedly. She slipped her feet into the soft, furry slippers and wiggled them, delighting in the animated way the bears moved. The slippers were huge.

"Her name is Lacey Winter. Her husband and I had some real-estate dealings. Now they're good friends of mine. You wouldn't believe the ridiculous-looking pair of clown slippers she made for her husband to wear. She put hours of hand sewing into them, and they're the neatest, goofiest things I've ever seen."

"He must really love her if he doesn't mind clown slippers."

King nodded. "He used to be a very straight-arrow business type, but on their first date she got him to wear a T-shirt with a clown on it. Clowns have been an inside joke between them ever since. They have a crazy, wonderful relationship."

Kaylyn heard the yearning in King's voice, and she wondered if he envied his friends' happiness. "These slippers would be terrific for the residents of the nursing home," she said. "I'll have to get Lacey's phone number and call her."

"You'll like her. She's a great gal."

King got a thick hand towel from the kitchen, walked behind the chair Kaylyn was sitting in, and began drying her hair. His motions were slow and rhythmic, and she felt her scalp begin to tingle.

"I adore Lacey's children," he murmured.

"Oh? How many does she have?"

"Three. And the last time I saw her and her husband, they said they aren't done yet."

"They must have a very happy family. I can tell that you envy them."

He paused for a moment. "Yes, I guess I do. My father died when I was young."

"So did mine. Or at least I've been told that he did. He ran off, and my mother and I never heard from him again."

"It was my mother who ran away." His voice was gruff. "I was a little kid when she left."

Kaylyn turned around and caught his hands between hers. His fingers rested lightly against her temples. "I never heard from my father again. Did your mother ever return? I'm sorry, King," she murmured. "I didn't mean to pry."

"No, she died soon afterward, but I like to think that she would have come home someday. And you weren't prying," he said softly. "You were sympathizing."

His hands were callused, the skin coarse. Yet they were surprisingly gentle hands for a man so big and aggressive. He probably could have broken granite rocks with those hands, she thought, but right now they roamed over her face so tenderly, she felt as if butterflies were caressing her skin.

"I care about people," she said breathlessly. Silently she added, *I care about you.*

"I believe you truly do," he whispered, and lowered his head to touch her lips with his.

For a long, still moment he simply kissed her with the same butterfly lightness that she'd felt in his fingertips. He was waiting, questioning, and she couldn't force herself to pull away, not this time. She was only dimly aware of her hands sliding around his neck. She was less aware of his hands slipping down her back and fastening around her waist.

There was an empty ache in her chest. She felt as if she were waiting for him to overwhelm that ache with happiness. Her response frightened her because she knew she was in grave danger of giving in to her insatiable desire for King, and that desire might destroy everything she wanted to achieve.

She drew away, twisting herself around in the chair, away from his touch. She closed her eyes, trying to blot out the mental image of his stormy blue-gray eyes and his lips parted invitingly.

"King," she asked sadly, "why do you keep trying to seduce me? This isn't doing either of us any good."

"That's a true statement if I ever heard one." His voice was hoarse, and she knew he'd been as swamped with emotion as she. He walked over to the window and stared into the darkness. "The robe I loaned you the other day . . . why didn't you return it?"

"I—I was waiting for a good time."

"You like wearing it," he said huskily.

"How did you know that I've been . . ."

"I've seen you take your dawn swim in the pool. I've seen you put my robe on when you're finished."

She felt warmth rising up her neck. She'd forgotten that he could see her out the trailer window. "King Vandergriff, you Peeping Tom, you."

"Only in your case, darlin'."

The silence that descended was rife with meaning. King struggled to get his breathing under control. By pinning his attention on the sound of the rain on the trailer's aluminum roof, he hoped to sidetrack his urge to carry Kaylyn to his bedroom.

"Why didn't you join me at the springs?" she asked. "I thought you enjoyed provoking me."

He laughed dryly. Staying in the trailer had been the hardest discipline he'd ever forced on himself.

"At the time it didn't seem like a very smart idea," he answered. "I was taught in high-school history that consorting with the enemy is called treason."

"What do you call this situation tonight?" She bit her lip to hold back a nervous giggle. She never giggled. She never even had to consciously keep herself from giggling. But then, she'd never been half dressed in a small trailer with a man like King Vandergriff before.

He grinned crookedly. "This, Ms. Smith, is a temporary truce for humanitarian purposes."

"You mean humanitarian as in rescuing Harold and giving him meaningful work?"

"Exactly." He turned to face her. "And humanitarian as in feeding the homeless and taking in pregnant donkeys."

"Where does it say that kissing is a humanitarian act?" she asked quietly.

His eyes gleamed with amusement. "On the third page of the book on humanitarianism. Didn't you study that in school?"

"Of course. In the history text it's right after the page that says feed and—"

"Clothe," he interjected. "Feed and clothe the enemy in order to create diplomacy. I've done my part. When are you going to do yours?"

"Mine? Oh, yes. Feed the enemy." She stood nervously, tightening the belt of the velour robe.

"Whoa, darlin'. The kind of care *this* enemy craves doesn't have to do with food." He paused and his expression became serious. "It's physical and emotional. And I don't know what to do about it. Kaylyn . . . something's happening here, something very special. I'm not at all sure what we ought to do about it."

She tried desperately to sound nonchalant. "What's happening is that you're offering shelter to a rain-soaked woman." She changed the subject. "Sounds like the rain is tapering off. Maybe Luther and Sandi will be able to get the van over here in the morning, after all."

"Why? Do they need food and clothing too? Or . . . *I* know. Luther is the father of Sandi's unborn child, and Sandi has been turned out of the Pretty Springs Girls' Reformatory. She's in disgrace and broke, and Luther is bringing her to you because you're the most tenderhearted person he knows."

"My, my, Mr. Vandergriff! What an active imagination you have!" Kaylyn laughed. "Luther is seventy-seven years old, and Sandi is only twenty-nine. She is neither pregnant *nor* his girlfriend. At least I don't think so. She went out with your foreman last night, so I can't be sure, of course."

"She went out with Mac? Now, why doesn't that surprise me?"

"Mac is very nice, King, and so is Sandi."

"I'm very nice," he said slyly. "And *you're* very nice. Maybe *we* should go out on a date."

She made a gentle huffing sound that dismissed his teasing. "Don't you want me to heat up the soup for you?"

"No, Kaylyn." He walked over to her, put his hands on her shoulders, and kissed her very lightly, as thought he'd just discovered kissing and wanted to be careful not to bruise her mouth. "What I want," he whispered, "is to love you, to take that robe off that sweet body and put my seal of approval on every inch of you. What I want is to wake up in the morning with you in my arms. What do you want, Kaylyn?"

"No, King, no," she said shakily, stepping back. "We can't do this. What I want is to save the springs, finish the section for wild animals we're building over at the animal shelter, and start a mission for the homeless. The only personal thing I want is . . ."

"You want something for yourself? Just name it, Katie, and I'll give it to you tonight."

"I'm afraid it's not a good idea," she muttered.

"Speak, speak," he ordered in a deep, teasing voice.

She sighed. "What I really want," she admitted, "is for someone to rub lotion on my poison ivy." What she really wanted was for King to make good on every sensual word he'd spoken, but she wouldn't allow herself to think about *that.*

He threw back his head and laughed. "Kaylyn, darlin', do you know how tempting your request is?"

"Would you rub some lotion on my back? It's driving me crazy and I can't reach it."

He rolled his eyes. "Will this mean that we're engaged?"

"It means that I trust you to be a *responsible* doctor. Harold said you have some calamine lotion in your medicine cabinet."

"For once in his life Harold said the right thing. Come with me."

He took her hand and pulled her along a narrow corridor to the room at the end. "Just lie down and I'll get the lotion."

Kaylyn looked at his bed and began to laugh. It was big and it was red.

"What's so funny?"

"I've heard of *king*-size beds, but this is ridiculous."

"Well, I'm a big man, and it didn't seem to matter if there's room to walk. I told the builder to leave me just enough space to make the bed up."

Kaylyn eyed the room. An open door indicated a bath area on the far side of the bed. "He obviously ignored you. There's no place to stand."

"I just get in the middle and spread out the sheets from there. Let me see your rash, Kaylyn."

"I don't suppose you could do this in the dark, could you?"

"Kaylyn, darlin', if we turn out the lights, what we'll do in the dark won't have any effect on your poison ivy."

"Ah. Good point." She stretched out on her stomach on the bed and shrugged the robe down her back. King went into the bathroom and returned with a small bottle of pink liquid and climbed on the bed with her. He straddled her body with his powerful thighs and began spreading the lotion between her shoulder blades.

"Hmm, it's warm," she murmured. "I'm surprised."

"It was cold until it hit my hands," he said rakishly.

He caressed her back lightly, sliding his fingers across her shoulders and down her spine.

"You're tense," he said, following the corded muscles up the side of her neck and under the base of her skull. "Relax. I once knew a lady who had fingertips that could practically commune with the spinal column. Let me show you."

She took a deep breath. The fingers kneading her back were bringing new meaning to the term *show-and-tell.* She felt the heat emanating from his hands. It dug into her pores like the heat of the sun on a white-hot Florida beach in mid-July. And the heat skittered across her skin and down her legs, where she felt the slight, instinctive movement of her inner thighs.

"Thank you," she said. "I think I'm relaxed now, as relaxed as I'll ever be on this bed."

"Oh, no, you're not. Sooner or later you'll be much

more relaxed—on this very bed." His hands stopped and lay still on her back. She felt the rise and fall of his touch as he breathed. There was no mistaking his arousal, pressing hotly against her.

There was no mistaking the noise outside, either. Something large and probably expensive had crashed into something equally as large and probably just as expensive. King leapt off the bed and headed for the door to the hall. Kaylyn took a moment to pull his robe back over her shoulders and followed.

He threw the trailer door open, and she stopped beside it, watching him pull on rubber boots and a rain poncho. She peered out into the darkness, but all she could see was a frightened-looking Matilda.

"What is it, King?"

"I'm not sure, but it sounded like equipment crashing. You stay here. I'll check it out. I'll be right back."

But he didn't come right back, and when the rain stopped, Kaylyn stepped outside and listened to the distant sounds of machines moving. Mac, dirty and disheveled, walked by the trailer.

"What happened?" she asked.

"One of the men left a tractor out of gear. It rolled down a hill and into several other machines. King and I have a night's work cut out for us."

He politely avoided staring at her, but she knew that he was wondering what she and King had been doing inside the trailer. Feeling embarrassed and vulnerable, she went back inside and gathered her clothes. How in the world had she let herself get in this predicament tonight? she asked herself repeatedly. One more minute on the bed with King and she would have made love with him, not caring what happened to Pretty Springs or Lizard Rock or her goals.

She returned to her tent and huddled miserably in her damp sleeping bag. When sleep finally came, her dreams were vague and sad, as if she'd lost something that she'd never regain.

At dawn King came back to the trailer. He was exhausted. His boots were covered in mud, and his hair was slicked to his head with rain. Kaylyn was gone. Only the indention of her head on his pillow was evidence that they'd shared a few minutes of gentle, thrilling camaraderie. The pillow smelled of her, a wildflower fragrance. After he showered, he lay down on his stomach and burrowed his head against that fragrance.

His body's reaction to her scent was powerful and frustrating—too frustrating. He didn't need this kind of distraction. He'd never allowed anyone to sway him from his goals before, and last night Kaylyn had nearly done it. He realized with alarm that he'd been a heartbeat away from telling her he'd drop the whole construction project, and she could keep enjoying her beautiful springs and her whimsical notions about their healing powers.

He suddenly threw the pillow onto the floor. Later that day he had a new tent delivered to Ms. Kaylyn Smith, Humanitarian, Pretty Springs.

Four

"I don't know what to think, Sandi," Kaylyn said to her friend a few days later. "After all that happened—his arrest, Matilda, the storm, the equipment crash, and my sit-in—the man actually sent a new army tent to the springs the next morning."

Kaylyn was in the activities room preparing the bulletin board that announced the annual Fourth of July Pretty Springs Founders' Day Picnic. She should have been focusing on the perennial manpower shortage for the picnic's crews. All she could think about was King Vandergriff's black satin bathrobe.

Sandi Arnold was standing in the doorway, sipping a glass of iced tea as she watched Minnie Rakestraw next door in the therapy room gamely lifting a small weight with her good hand.

"Not only did he send a tent for me," Kaylyn went on, "but he had one of his men erect a temporary shelter for Matilda."

"The donkey?"

"Yes. And a supply of hay appeared the day after that."

"Well, personally I think any man who shows compassion for a donkey can't be all bad. Has he said anything?"

"No. I haven't . . . spoken to him since the night of the storm. He comes in very late. But he doesn't cross the rocks to my side of the camp until after I'm in bed."

"Whoa, now. After you're in bed?" Sandi swallowed hard. Kaylyn could see she was trying not to choke on the liquid that threatened to go down the wrong way. "Want to explain that?"

"He swims in the springs—every night."

"I see. He just walks past your tent every night, and you never say a word."

"That's right. He doesn't say anything, so why should I?"

"But you watch."

"Yes. I mean, well, he's swimming right next to the window in my tent. And he splashes around like some great whale in the moonlight."

"Great-looking guy, isn't he?" Sandi said casually, rolling her now empty glass in her hands.

"I suppose you could say that he's . . . attractive," Kaylyn admitted as she stepped back to survey the finished board.

"Yes, I suppose. If you call the most gorgeous specimen of manhood to hit this town in the three years I've been here 'attractive,' he'd qualify. I heard he looks great in red."

Kaylyn's chest constricted, and she tried to conceal a sudden gasp for breath with an obvious cough. "Well, yes. He does have rather interesting taste in clothing." Obviously Sandi was referring to King's red socks and underwear that first day on the rock.

"You can tell that in the dark, can you?"

Kaylyn didn't answer. She opened the supply cabinet to begin assembling the games and craft materials for the afternoon activities session. Discussing King Vandergriff was making her uncomfortable.

Sandi walked over to the bulletin board. "Say, Katie, have you thought about asking King to the Founders' Day Picnic?"

"Me? Invite King Vandergriff to the picnic? What earthly reason would I have for doing that?"

"I don't know. It just occurred to me that he might enjoy getting to know some of the townspeople."

"Introduce him to Pretty Springs . . . Great Jehoshaphat! Wait a minute. Maybe that isn't such a bad idea, Sandi. If I could involve him on a personal basis, he'd get to meet Minnie, Luther, and the others. He'd see what his Golf and Tennis Club would destroy. I'll bet my last penny that he's never been to a town picnic."

"Well, that isn't exactly what I had in mind," Sandi said dryly. "Have you considered the possibility that he might like to go to the dance with you?"

"With me? Why?"

"Come on, Kaylyn. Sometimes I think you fell off a turnip truck. It's possible that the man's interested in *you*—not the fine citizens of Pretty Springs. Besides, if you take him to the dance, Minnie will win two dollars."

"What? Why will Minnie win two dollars if I invite King to the Founders' Day Dance?"

"The nursing-home residents have decided that

you and his highness are perfect for each other. They all sat down and put money in the pot. Then they mapped out the course of the romance, and each of them drew events. Minnie got the dance, and the dance paid two dollars."

"Oh, lordy, they're betting on our having a romance? What other events have they planned for me?"

"Well," Sandi admitted, "I missed the end of the session, so I don't know everything, but you know how romantic this group is."

Kaylyn knew about the nursing-home residents, all right. She'd lived in the nursing home itself for the first year, then in her own small trailer parked behind the home for the last three. The residents were like her family. And they weren't above helping her with her latest project. She was still worried about the stray cat that the residents had managed to conceal from the management for over a year.

Kaylyn quickly gave Sandi the instructions for the afternoon crafts session. She was going to be late getting back to the springs. She had cooked the day's soup while Sandi exercised the patients in the springs that morning, but she knew that Tom Brolin would be there with the men before she arrived.

"By the way," Sandi called out as Kaylyn got into the van, "if you should happen to see Mac, you could tell him about the Founders' Day Picnic too."

"You wouldn't be looking for a date, would you?"

Sandi blushed. "Of course not. I just thought that maybe he'd volunteer his men to help us get all these busybodies to the barbecue."

"Good idea," Kaylyn said. "They might even agree to help set up everything."

All the way back to the springs she turned the idea over in her mind. First she'd get King to the picnic. If her plan to involve him with the nursing-home residents didn't work, at least she would drum up support for her cause by making the citizens aware of the man who was destroying the springs. Maybe public opinion could do what she hadn't been able to.

And if she could get the construction workers to . . . A solution to the manpower shortage began to take shape. If she could recruit enough men to set up the events, the stage, and the bleachers, then the fire and police departments need not be pulled from their regular duties. If the construction workers joined in, then maybe . . . just maybe . . .

"Well, what do you think, fellas?" Kaylyn asked. "Will you do it?"

Harold, who had become a regular member of her soup line, voiced the first question. "Are you sure that your fine citizens will want us 'bums' involved in their little celebration?"

"Yeah," an elderly man said. "Every time I've seen a policeman for the last three months, he's either been arresting me for vagrancy or telling me to move on."

"It would be nice to go to a real picnic with real families again," another man said wistfully

"What would you need us to do?" someone else asked.

Tom Brolin answered. "The picnic is on Saturday. The day before, we'll set up a stage for the band and the speakers, and some stands where the older residents and Kaylyn's folks from the nursing home can sit and watch the activities."

"I heard they have a three-legged race. Is that so, Ms. Smith?"

"Right you are," Kaylyn said. "The morning of the picnic we lay out the mud hole for the tug-of-war and set up the course for the three-legged race. Then we put up the picnic tables and cook the barbecue and Brunswick stew. You can see that we could certainly use your help."

From his trailer across the pool, King watched and listened through an open window as Kaylyn worked her magic. In no time she'd convinced a bunch of down-on-their-luck men to supply the manpower for the local Fourth of July picnic. If anybody else had come up with the idea, it probably would have been nixed on the drawing board. But King had no doubt that Kaylyn would bring it off. She was some woman.

The men began to venture suggestions. Soon they allowed themselves a guarded enthusiasm about the upcoming event. Enthusiasm and purpose were wonderful things, King knew. They changed a bunch of ex-bums into men with a quest. There'd been a time when he'd had no enthusiasm, and no purpose, either. Yet he'd pulled himself up by his boot straps and made his own way, and so had his brothers. Diamond, his sister, was getting there too.

What he didn't understand was Kaylyn Smith. Watching her stand back and allow the men to offer suggestions on how they could utilize their talents, he found it hard to condemn her for interfering with his project. He ought to throw her off the property.

The news media's interest in the protest had died down in light of the firm support of the city council. Kaylyn's eviction from the building site was unlikely to cause him any more bad press.

Truthfully, she intrigued him. In the five days she'd been at the springs, he'd found a dozen excuses to drop by his trailer during the day. When her campsite was empty, he was disappointed. When she was there, he alternated between anger at her for occupying his mind when he should be concentrating on the job, and the simple joy at watching her as she performed routine chores under primitive conditions.

He'd have a talk with her later, he thought. By now she must know that her protest wasn't doing any good. The symbolic picketing every afternoon by her soup-line regulars and a few nursing-home residents in wheelchairs didn't attract much attention outside of the pages of the *Pretty Springs Gazette*, and even Tom Brolin was running out of reasons to cover the event.

He'd invite her to dinner and discuss the situation with her sensibly. Then later they'd come back to the springs and . . . Later would take care of itself.

Kaylyn's tent was dark as King made his way to the springs. He wasn't quite sure why he'd made the icy midnight swim a nightly routine. The water was as cold as a witch's—well, it didn't compare with a good hot shower in the trailer. He'd intended to stroll over to her tent as soon as everyone left and have a simple conversation with her, but she'd gone off with Tom and Harold. He'd had to wait. Now he was hungry and tired and, he admitted, even a little jealous.

As he passed the tent window he paused, allowing himself to glance inside. But the interior was dark, as it was every night. She was probably already asleep and unaware of his midnight visits. He didn't know why he was so irritated at her indifference. She was trouble. He was better off ignoring her completely. He stood, torn by indecision. What he wanted to do was jerk the tent flap back, march inside her tent, and . . . hell, he didn't even know if she was in there.

The only sound he heard was the soft gurgle of the water as it churned to the surface. He had to admit that there was something physically and spiritually soothing about the sound, something good about knowing that the springs and that old Lizard had been there for two hundred thousand years. No matter how tired or out of sorts he was, he could work out his frustrations with his swim and sleep like a baby afterward. He felt his stomach muscles contract into hard knots. That night, especially, he hoped Kaylyn was right about the calming effects of the water.

He walked on, determined to bring his raging emotions under control. Soon his brother, Jack, the architect, would be there to help lay out the houses and the sites for the golf and tennis courts. Then Joker would be along to set up the memberships and handle the actual running of the community. How on earth was he going to explain Kaylyn Smith and a donkey camped out on the site?

He stubbed his toe and stumbled forward, trying to regain his balance. His bare foot hit a sharp sliver of rock, and it penetrated with a vengeance. "Ouch!" He hopped around on his good foot as he tried to bite back the pain. "Damn! Now the rocks are attacking."

Kaylyn had heard him thrashing in the darkness. Now she heard his oath and his genuine cry of pain. Without a thought she rushed from her tent to his side. "Who's attacking you? What's wrong?"

"It's sabotage. One of your rocks has stabbed me in the foot." He groaned, balancing himself by sliding his arm around her neck.

"Foot?" The word hung in the air as she felt the shock of his bare body against her. She didn't have to ask if his wardrobe was coordinated that night. The answer would have been no. No, that was wrong. The answer would have been yes. His feet were bare, and the rest of him matched perfectly.

"Here, sit down on the rock," she said thickly, "and let me get a light so that I can see."

"I don't think that's such a good idea," he said dryly.

She ignored him, tucked her shoulder under his arm, and helped him over to one of the large boulders. "Does it hurt bad?"

"No," he said bravely, sorry that she'd moved away. Kaylyn's height continually undermined his control. He'd never been with a woman as tall as she, and he found the experience unsettling. "I think it's just a flesh wound, just a warning from the Lizard."

"Wait here." She hurried back into the tent and reappeared with a lantern. She placed it on the ground and examined his foot. He hadn't been faking the injury as she'd suspected. There was no mistaking the seeping red blood that was staining the dirt beneath his foot.

"I give up. I'm dying," he said dramatically, openly ogling the woman kneeling before him. "You and the rocks have won."

"Shut up, Vandergriff. You easily could pick up blood poisoning from a wound like this."

Wound? He had long forgotten the cut. From the moment he had seen Kaylyn in the light of her lantern, his pain had disappeared. That wasn't a nightgown she was sleeping in. It was a man's worn white T-shirt, and it made a perfect second skin for the body beneath it. For five days he'd tried to block out the memory of her body as he'd seen it the first day on that damn rock. But the picture had been with him every minute since. And now she was perched invitingly before him. He moved slightly as the rough rock ground into his bottom.

"Is the pain bad?" she asked.

"Awful," he said, knowing the pain he was feeling had nothing to do with his foot.

"I think what we need to do is get your foot in the springs and clean out the dirt. Then I'll bandage it so you can get home."

He groaned. "You'll have to help me over to the springs."

"I know." She moved the lantern away and held out her hand, focusing her attention somewhere just above the head of the golden-haired man. She concentrated on Matilda, enjoying her shed out there in the darkness. For once the donkey was not straining to get close to King. For once Kaylyn would have welcomed the interruption.

He took her hand and rose, grabbing on to her as he wobbled unsteadily on one foot.

She tried to marshal her energy toward moving King to the pool, but his fingers, now digging into her shoulder, were setting off a vibration so strong that her teeth were chattering.

"I'm sorry," he said as they reached the pool. "I'm a little light-headed." He lurched around and sat down heavily, throwing Kaylyn off-balance and pulling her into his lap with a thud.

She steadied herself and tilted her head back to look up at him, trying desperately not to reveal her awareness of his nudity. "You're probably losing too much blood. If you'll lift your foot into the water, I'll get into the pool and take care of the problem."

"The problem isn't in the pool, Kaylyn Smith, the problem is out here." King felt a dizzying wave of passion sweep over him, and all thought of teasing Kaylyn disappeared. He wanted this woman. She was driving him wild with the wanting. For five days he'd suppressed his intense desire, and he couldn't hold back any longer. He wanted to touch her. He wanted to taste her. He bent his head and kissed her.

Kaylyn moaned a muffled no, but she didn't move away. He was storming her resistance once more. She was being torn apart by his very touch. And now his lips were setting off new waves of longing. When his tongue slipped inside her mouth, her mind stopped recording anything but the feel and touch of this man. He worked one hand beneath her T-shirt and cupped her bare breast. She kissed him back hungrily, every part of her responding magically to his touch.

His body was hard, and she felt the evidence of his desire pressed against her thigh. With her last ounce of reason she shifted, trying to escape from the part of him throbbing against her. Her foot grazed his and she felt his involuntary reaction as he moved it away. She also felt the sticky, warm pool beneath it.

She jerked her head back. "Your foot."

"Cut the damn thing off," he said savagely, then pulled her close again. His lips trailed fire down her neck, and he captured the budding nipple, shirt and all, inside his mouth.

"King!" she cried, knowing that if she didn't stop him now, she wouldn't stop at all. "King!" She shoved against a rock and toppled both of them into the icy waters of the springs.

"Damn, woman! You sure know how to put out a fire, don't you?"

"No," she said weakly as her feet touched bottom. "This is the first internal combustion I've ever encountered. This is virgin territory to me."

Virgin? He was at a loss for words. "Really?" Surely she was only making a comment. There was no way that a woman like Kaylyn could have managed to avoid some man's bed.

"Please, King, turn around and sit on the side so that you can swish your foot back and forth. While you wash the dirt out of the cut I'll get a sock to cover it. Then I'll help you back to your trailer so I can bandage it."

"Kaylyn, I don't think I can get back to my trailer.

Maybe I'd better just try to make it to your tent. It's big enough for two. I made certain of that."

"Oh?" Her heart leapt up into her throat. "Why would you do that?" She eased out of the pool, embarrassed at how her wet T-shirt molded to her body.

"I wasn't sure. But the way you were going, I thought you might be about to open a hotel along with your soup kitchen."

In the moonlight she was the loveliest thing he had ever seen. She was a legend come to life. She was the maiden pure and sweet, waiting in the forest for the unicorn. The night, the springs, everything about Kaylyn Smith was magic. And she had no idea. Of all the weapons she had available to influence him, she'd made no attempt to use the one most likely to work—herself.

She disappeared into the tent, then reappeared carrying a thick white athletic sock and his red robe. "Here, let me help you out." She reached down and offered her hand.

He refused. If he took her hand, he'd just pull her into the springs again. What he wanted right now was to be standing close to her, or lying close to her, or having her beneath him. . . . He shook off that image and lifted himself from the water, being careful not to touch the hurt foot to the ground.

Kaylyn quickly slid the sock over his foot, keeping her gaze away from his body. She knew she was almost as nude as he, knew he was staring at her. He wasn't even trying to look away. She took a deep breath and held out the red robe. "Put this on."

"You're returning my robe . . . now?"

"I'm returning your robe . . . now. I think you can

get back to your trailer without getting the wound dirty again."

"You're going to send a wounded man out into the darkness? Not Kaylyn Smith, the angel of mercy to all those at home and on the ships at sea? I think I'd better lie down instead—in your tent."

"Cut the dramatics, Vandergriff. I'll get you back to your trailer if I have to carry you." She took his hand and pulled him up to a standing position, then slid her arm under his and around his back. With the Amazonlike strength of one used to lifting patients, she walked him forcefully across the campsite and back to his trailer.

"Careful, Smith," he said teasingly, sliding his own arm across her body with an exaggerated need to steady himself. That his hand chose her breast to anchor itself was a fact she didn't acknowledge as they stumbled up on his porch. "This time," he went on, "I'm the one who could have you arrested for assault with a deadly weapon."

"Arrested?" She chortled. "What kind of deadly weapon could I possibly have when I'm standing here wearing only a T-shirt?"

"Aside from the rocks under your control, there's this." He lowered his head once more, and before she realized what he was doing, he'd recaptured her nipple in his mouth and began to suck.

"Stop that, King! Get your lips off my—my body, or I'll sic Matilda on you."

"Tell Matilda to get her own man. I'm already taken." He moved to the other breast and gave it the same kind of attention.

"King, please!" she whimpered. "Please! I want to

talk to you, not make love to you. At least not now. I mean . . . Oh, King."

He was kissing her again. His robe had come untied, and her T-shirt was suddenly bunched above her waist. Her body was being cupped from behind and lifted into the evidence of his desire. And she was kissing him back. She felt his arousal slide between her legs and undulate hard against her. He didn't enter her. He didn't have to. He was bringing her to the full peak of desire without it.

"Oh, King. Please stop. We have issues to settle. Please."

"We're settling them," he whispered. He opened the door and lifted her inside. "This is called negotiating a settlement. Cooperate, my darlin' Kay. Please."

"Are you saying that if I let you make love to me, you'll give up closing the springs? Would that satisfy you?"

He stopped. His hands left her body. His head drew back, and the hard part of him between her legs slid away.

"You'd agree to that?" His voice was cold and strange.

"Yes! No! I—I don't know. I just want to be certain I understand what you meant."

"You would, wouldn't you? You'd make love to me to settle the issue, wouldn't you?"

Kaylyn was floundering now. Her body was protesting King's sudden withdrawal. Her mind was trying desperately to reclaim control from her emotions. She wasn't even sure what she was saying, certainly not what King was so harshly suggesting. She only knew that she had to get away before she ended up in his bed.

"Maybe," she said breathlessly, "if you'd give me a guarantee that you'd live up to your word. Oh, I don't mean that. King, I'm sorry. I don't know what I mean. You move too fast for me. I never got past . . ." She began to laugh. "Can you imagine, I'm lying there in my tent trying to figure out how I can invite you to attend the Founders' Day Picnic, and you've already got me in your bed? See how far apart we are? I'm planning to ask you for a date, and you're planning an orgy. Silly me."

"I accept."

"You what?"

"I said, I accept. I'll be your date for the picnic."

"You will?"

"I will."

"But why?"

"Why? Hell, I don't know, and right now I don't think we'd better start any long, drawn-out discussions. I'm holding onto my control by a thread, Kaylyn Smith, and I don't think you're in much better shape."

"You'll really go?" she asked in disbelief, watching him retie the sash on his red robe.

"Yes, I'll really go. Now get your sweet tush out of here before I overwhelm you. I think you must be in touch with some leftover Indian spirits. I'm still not too sure about that runaway bulldozer. Mac swears he checked it. And now I've cut my foot on a rock? No, darlin'. I don't think this little trailer could withstand a rock slide, and I don't trust those boulders out there for one minute."

Kaylyn smiled. "I tried to tell you that this place is special." She gave the iron-faced man a quick kiss, then danced out into the night.

In the moonlight the rocks gleamed like polished silver. The springs gurgled in contentment, and in the distance the Lizard seemed relaxed in sleep. But Kaylyn wasn't fooled for a minute. He was on her side. King was right. She'd always felt the benevolent presence of the Cherokee Indian spirits here. She'd sensed their approval from the beginning—even if nobody else did.

Five

"He's even sent a Bobcat over here to dig the mud hole for the tug-of-war," Tom said to Kaylyn. Clipboard in hand, he was standing on the newly completed speaker's platform watching the viewers' stand take shape.

"A cat? Wouldn't a shovel be easier?"

"A Bobcat is a little machine, Kaylyn. The Pretty Springs Founders' Day Picnic has taken a giant leap into the twenty-first century, thanks to King Vandergriff. What do you think of the stands?"

"They don't look like temporary structures to me," she said. Mac and his construction crew were setting up massive pieces of lumber and nailing them into place, hurrying to get the work done before the celebration began that afternoon. She was beginning to get a bad feeling about the outcome she'd envisioned. "Why have you changed the direction of its view?"

"Because the stands aren't temporary. King said

that if they were going to build seats, they might as well build something to last. It will be a gift from Vandergriff, Inc., to Pretty Springs. He's even building a handicapped ramp for your wheelchair group."

"Great!" Kaylyn said dryly. "Here I'm trying to present him to the world as someone only interested in commercialism, and he's looking more and more like King Arthur. I don't see him. Where is he, out shaking hands and kissing babies?"

"He took your soup-line crew out to breakfast."

"The soup-line crew?" King Vandergriff's actions were growing more bizarre by the minute. "To breakfast?"

"By the way," Tom added proudly, "your idea about having the men from the soup line help with the picnic has worked out even better than you thought. The church members who've supplied the food have decided to cook and serve it in their kitchen from now on. So you don't have to run a restaurant anymore. There's even some talk about trying to find homes and jobs for these men."

"Wonderful," she said as she surveyed the picnic site with amazement. "You and I work year after year to make a few changes—without any substantial results, I might add—and King Vandergriff gets involved and things begin to happen. It must be nice to have so much power. I hope he enjoys the adoration."

"What's the matter, Katie? King turning out to have more of a heart that you'd expected?"

"I sound like the town's most ungrateful citizen, don't I? It isn't that I'm not appreciative. I just wonder about motives."

From the time the "soupies," as they'd begun to

call themselves, and the construction crew had reported for work the previous day, the townspeople had welcomed them. Kaylyn had no doubt that their combined efforts would make this celebration the best Pretty Springs had ever had. One thing she hadn't counted on was turning King into a hero.

She couldn't find a single fault with either King or his crew, or the homeless who were finding a purpose and an acceptance that they hadn't believed possible. Why, then, was she feeling so out of sorts? Everything was working out the way she'd wanted, wasn't it? But she'd known that from the beginning. Why was it suddenly so hard for her to accept the very results she'd anticipated?

It was King. Why was he doing this? she wondered. Would his kindnesses to the town cost her Lizard Rock and the use of the springs? Was he sincere in what he was doing, or was this some kind of ploy? Since he'd hurt his foot a few days ago, he hadn't come back to the springs for a swim. Harold had refused to discuss his employer's health or his whereabouts. King was ignoring her completely. She didn't know what she'd expected, but she hadn't expected him to give up. He wasn't the type. She'd thought he might at least speak to her, try to see her, maybe even attempt to kiss her again. Not knowing where he was or what he was thinking was making her as jumpy as a cat.

"Hello, darlin'."

The Stetson and alligator boots were back. And the man wearing them was as heart-stoppingly gorgeous as he'd been that first day when she'd watched him approach Lizard Rock.

"Good morning, Mr. Vandergriff. Your men certainly are doing a fine job here."

"Yes, they are, aren't they, Ms. Smith? Since we got the site lined up properly, it's been a piece of cake."

"What do you mean, lined up properly?"

"No reflection on you, Kaylyn, darlin', but whoever arranged the placement of the events had no concept of efficient design. The layout was a confusing mishmash. The tug-of-war in the middle of the walking space between the booths? We moved it over there so that the mud hole would be out of the way." He pointed to a section near the wooden booths being erected for goods to be sold for various charities.

"But it's always been in the center of the walking space," she said, trying to curb the anger she felt at his high-handed interference.

"Why?"

"Because . . . because . . . oh, I don't know. Tradition, I guess."

"Well, it won't be there anymore. And neither will the course for the three-legged race. We've moved it to the other side of the tug-of-war. That way we can build permanent stands that are perfect for viewing the fireworks, plus watching the street dance in the square. By turning slightly, the crowd can see the race and the tug-of-war as well. What do you think?"

"I think," she admitted with a queer pain twisting her insides like an old-fashioned wringer washing machine, "that you've really got all this arranged. Nothing like having an engineer around to point out the errors of our planning. You've done a good job. I can't see a thing for me to do, so I'll take off. Thank you, Mr. Vandergriff."

She managed a two-fingered salute of approval to Tom as she headed back to the nursing home van. She wasn't needed here. With Harold manning the barbecue, Tom overseeing the activities, and King and his crew doing the physical labor, she could go back to her trailer and . . . and do what? She wasn't quite sure. She'd never had the luxury of free time before.

She'd almost reached the van when she felt two strong arms circle her waist from behind and lift her easily from the ground.

"Now, darlin', you just hang on there a minute. I'm wearing all my clothes. I've brought my entire crew over here to help out on your little project, and I've put Harold in charge of the cooking. I've done everything I could think of to please you, and you're not leaving here with that burr under your saddle. What's wrong?"

"Put me down, King Vandergriff. Everyone is watching."

"Not until we talk. Let them watch. Now, either you come with me or I'll carry you off with the approval of everybody here. You've never been shy before. Do you need a television camera on you before you'll discuss a problem?"

"That's cruel—and it isn't true."

He kept on walking, holding her feet off the ground.

"All right, King, put me down. We'll talk."

He lowered her to the ground, reluctantly sliding his hands away from her waist. She smelled like flowers. Her hair was tousled by the wind. The usual T-shirt she was wearing was spotted on the back with perspiration. He didn't want to let her go. So what was new about that? Every time he saw her it was harder to keep from touching her.

She turned to face him, smiled at the curious onlookers, and took his arm in hers, as if he were simply walking her to the van. "But," she said, her lips curved in a false smile, "if you really wanted to talk to me, why have you avoided me for the past three days?"

"Oh, you don't like being ignored?"

For the benefit of those watching, she widened her smile until her face hurt. She wiped a bead of perspiration that had rimmed her cheek and was about to run down her neck. "Leave me alone, cowboy."

"Why, darlin'." He returned her forced smile with one of amusement and tipped his hat to Esther Hainey, who was driving by in the Humane Society station wagon. As they reached the van he deftly dropped Kaylyn's arm and leaned one hand against the door on the driver's side, effectively preventing her from getting inside. "I believe you missed me."

"Not a chance, buster. If you really wanted to talk, why wait until now? Does it take a public display of adoration to reach you?"

"The last I noticed, it was the same number of steps from my trailer to your tent as it was from your tent to my trailer. And so far you haven't impressed me with your shyness. What's your excuse?"

"It wasn't shyness," she said, moving away from him, "it was shock. You as much as made me a proposition that if I'd sleep with you, you'd let me keep the springs."

Resting his other hand on the van, he imprisoned her inside his arms. His smile narrowed into a straight line of displeasure. "Not sleep with me, Kaylyn. You and I will sleep together one day. But sleeping isn't what we were talking about. Correct me if I'm wrong, but what we were discussing was your trading the use of your body for those springs, wasn't it?"

One by one the sounds of construction behind them came to a stop. Kaylyn refused to look. She knew that every man and woman in the park was watching. Her pulse was racing, and her lungs felt as if she'd already taken in the last breath of oxygen in the atmosphere. And King? He stood over her, daring her to argue. He wasn't touching her, yet her body felt every part of him as though it were pressed against him.

"Does this mean," he asked, "that you're more important to yourself than those springs are to your patients?"

King groaned silently at his own words. He knew better than that. Why was he doing this? He had expected her to be pleased with what he was doing. Dammit, what had gone wrong? He'd made all these charitable gestures for her. Why was she looking up at him with such pain in her eyes? He'd expected her to fling herself into his arms and rain kisses all over his face.

Even now a bottle of champagne was chilling in his trailer. For days he'd been planning. He'd take her to the dance that night, and afterward they'd go back to his trailer and make love. Instead, here she was, eyes flashing fire, her breathing fast and furious, staring at him as if he'd suddenly grown a tail. And he was making hurtful accusations about bartering sex for the springs.

"Let me go, King. I don't know how to play games. You confuse me." Kaylyn knew that her anger wasn't because he was redesigning the town square. What he'd planned was much better than her past efforts. She was bothered by his self-confidence and the easy way he'd taken over and ingratiated himself with the people.

Calling him the outsider who didn't fit in had suited her purposes. But now he belonged, and she was torn between pride in what he was accomplishing for the celebration and despair at the crumbling of her plans to save the springs. It all came down to motives. She wasn't at all sure about her own. The man kept getting mixed up with her emotions, and she was very confused.

As they stood there like dolls with magnets inside them, their bodies straining to join, she could feel a current arcing between them like an electrical charge. His expression suddenly changed. He smiled again, and the smile wasn't forced.

"Don't be afraid, Kaylyn. We've got to learn how to be together. This is all new to me too. We just have to let it happen." His head was lowering, and she knew he was going to kiss her. In the middle of the town square, with everybody watching, he was going to kiss her.

"Don't, King. Don't. This won't solve anything. You mustn't kiss me now."

"Why not, darlin'? I want to kiss you now. My whole body is crying out to kiss you now." His lips were moving closer.

"Because! Because," she said wildly, "Minnie Rakestraw will lose her money if you do."

He blinked and drew back in surprise. "What?"

"Minnie has a kiss at the dance for two dollars."

"Who's Minnie, and who's betting?"

"Minnie is one of my favorite patients," Kaylyn said rapidly. "She and Luther and the others at the nursing home have a betting pool on our romance. She drew the dance. If you and I go to the dance together and you kiss me, she wins two dollars."

King shook his head. "And I thought Joker was a gambler. We'll have to introduce him to Minnie."

"Who's Joker?"

"Joker's my brother. Being a practical joker is what got him his name, but there's one thing he likes better than playing jokes. Gambling. I'll introduce him to you when he gets here."

"I'd like that." She spoke without even being certain what she was saying. Anything to distract King from kissing her in front of the whole town.

"All right, darlin'," he said, letting his arms fall to his sides. "I'll take a rain check on the kiss. We wouldn't want to disappoint Miss Minnie. What time do I pick you up for the picnic?"

"You really don't have to pick me up. I just wanted you to get to know the townspeople. I thought you'd probably never been to anything like this before."

"Well, normally I'd be running in the Peachtree Road Race in Atlanta on the Fourth of July, but I passed that up for the three-legged race—and you, darlin'. I intend to spend the entire day with you and take you to the dance tonight as well. We'll have a date, lady. We've got to win two dollars for Miss Minnie."

Kaylyn straightened her shoulders. She couldn't handle the man. He was like quicksilver, sliding from one outrageous thing to the next. "But why? If all this help is to win support for your side, you've already accomplished that."

"My side? Is that what you think I'm doing? All right, I'll admit that I might have started out that way. But you know what? I've found out that I like being able to do something worthwhile. It makes me feel good. That isn't wrong, is it?"

"No, I guess not," she admitted. "It's me who's being selfish. I do appreciate your help. What you've done is grand. I'm sorry, King. Now I've got to get back to the nursing home and set everything up to bring the ambulatory residents to the picnic."

"No you don't. Not this time. Sandi and Mac will take care of that. It's already arranged."

"I see. You've thought of everything. In that case, pick me up at the trailer parked behind the nursing home at twelve o'clock."

"Nursing home? You're not leaving the tent, are you? What about the springs and Matilda?"

"I'm not clearing out yet, King. It's just that my clothes are at my trailer. And Matilda has enough food and water to last until tomorrow. But you could check on her when you get back, if you don't mind. And, by the way, Tom told me that the church is going to move the soup line to their kitchen. You won't be bothered anymore."

"I know. But you aren't giving up your protest, are you?" He lowered his voice. "I like knowing that I have an audience for my midnight swim. It won't be the same without you over there in that tent. And I'll never get started in the morning without my sunrise shot of adrenaline."

She opened the van door and climbed inside. "What sunrise shot of adrenaline?"

"Oh, I always have a cup of coffee as I watch you take your morning swim. Gets the old body up and going, no pun intended, darlin'."

"Oh, you!" she slammed the van door shut. "Don't you ever think about anything but your body?"

"Yes, indeedy." He reached his hand through the open window and ran it down her chest, stopping to take her nipple between his thumb and forefinger. "I think a great deal about your body, Ms. Smith." He stared at her breast. "Would you look at that?"

Kaylyn started the engine and gunned it loudly. She didn't have to look. She could feel her traitorous body coming to life beneath his touch. Her nipple had peaked and hardened, and the ripples of delight radiating from his touch were making her body feel like a marshmallow on a stick at a wiener roast.

"Get away from this van, King, or your brother, Joker, will be attending a funeral—yours."

"Certainly, Kaylyn," he said cheerfully, and stepped away from the van. "By the way, do you know any of the rest of the wagers? I'd like to know what's in the nursing-home pool so that we can plot the course of our romance. After all, we might as well give them something to look forward to."

"There is no romance, King. There is only an issue to be settled. The springs and Lizard Rock, remember?"

"Oh, I remember, all right, but you're dead wrong about the romance. However, we'll leave that until later. I'll pick you up in a few hours. And, I promise you, darlin', I'll never forget the Lizard."

He was late. It was almost twelve-thirty when

Kaylyn opened the door to her trailer and King stepped inside, filling every inch of the door frame. He was dressed in faded jeans, a pale pink polo shirt, and well-worn sneakers.

"Where're your boots?" she asked.

"I thought it might be easier to win the race in these."

"Not the three-legged race. You're really entered in that race?"

"I sure am. But it's not me, it's we. I've even got a bet or two going myself. Harold says the odds are changing every hour."

"I don't know what you did to Harold. I figured by now he'd have fallen off the wagon and reclaimed his cell at the jail permanently."

"Harold? Not on your life. He's totally reformed. Since he's representing my interests, he's become downright stuffy. This morning he even had breakfast with the mayor and the town council to discuss the day's activities."

"Imagine that."

"Yes, indeed. Everybody is involved in your Founders' Day celebration this year."

"Including my patients," she said dryly. Behind him, in her driveway, she could see a shiny black Ferrari. And behind the Ferrari she could see a head in every window of the nursing home.

"You'd better not come in," she said, nodding toward the home. "Our voyeurs won't know what we're doing, and they'll probably send over a messenger to find out whether we're kissing."

"Well, let's not keep them in suspense, darlin'." He swept her into his arms, and before she could protest, he was kissing her. She hadn't realized how much she'd wanted to be kissed until his lips touched hers and she melted into his body.

"What about Minnie's money?" she whispered.

"I'll pay her myself."

"You have a fetish for kissing, don't you, King?"

"Not just kissing in general. Kissing *you*, Kaylyn, darlin'."

He kissed her again, she kissed him back, and all her plans to keep her distance and pretend she was having a date with a vampire went straight up in smoke.

Finally, amid a smattering of clapping and a whistle or two, Kaylyn pulled away. "King, please. I wish you wouldn't keep doing that. If we're going to spend the entire day together, couldn't we pretend we're strangers, or that we're on a first date or something?"

"We are. This is our first date, and I'm definitely looking forward to the something, as long as you let me plan it. May I tell you how lovely you are today?"

He took her hand as he stepped back, so he could give her a thorough once-over. "I really prefer the string bikini or the cutoffs, but this is nice."

She was wearing a cherry-colored cotton sundress with a ruffle at the hem and along the straps. On her feet she wore simple flat matching leather shoes. Her hair was a mass of golden curls. Peeking out from beneath the curls were huge golden hoops threaded through her ears. Matching gold bands jangled on her wrist. All in all, he thought she looked like a wild Gypsy. He felt his pulse quicken as he squeezed her hand.

"Just for today, Kaylyn, couldn't we pretend we really are on a date? I'm a boy and you're a girl, and it's the Fourth of July. And you're right. I've never been to a Founders' Day Picnic before. Are they fun?"

There was something so little-boy-like about his enthusiasm, something she couldn't resist. Why not? she asked herself. She'd never had a date for the Founders' Day Picnic before. Suddenly she felt a lighthearted bubble of laughter threatening to escape. She wasn't used to mood changes. She wasn't used to having a man hold her hand. She didn't know the rules.

"I don't know if they're fun," she said honestly. "I've always been so busy that I've never actually been to the picnic as a spectator."

"Will you go with me to the barbecue, Miss Kaylyn, be my lady for the day?" He backed off the porch and down the steps to the ground and waited, still holding her hand.

"Why, Mr. Vandergriff, sir, I'd be delighted." She pulled the trailer door closed behind her and allowed him to seat her in his sports car.

He started the engine, glancing up at the nursing home windows and back at Kaylyn with a smile as warm as the midday sunshine. As he turned the car around and came back even with the nursing home, he bowed his head like an actor taking a curtain call, making a dramatic sweeping gesture toward the windows. Then he touched the car horn and hit the gas, roaring off in a trail of loose gravel and dust.

"You're a ham," she said. "At least you've given them something to talk about. They probably all have heart palpitations. Poor things. They aren't even going to get to go to the picnic."

"Not to worry, Kaylyn Smith. Right about now

they're drinking iced tea made from your famous mineral water. It will cushion their stomachs for Harold's barbecue sauce. I have it on good authority that spring water will lower the blood pressure and calm the soul."

"Ah, so I'm making a believer out of you."

"Not on your life. My blood pressure is threatening to explode, and my other parts aren't doing any better. And that's after drinking two tall glasses of that foul-tasting water before I came to pick you up."

"What can I say, your highness? It works for me."

"Uh-huh. Me drinking water from your springs and expecting it to keep me calm when you're around me is like trying to treat poison ivy when you're standing in it. By the way, how's your rash?"

"Gone, thanks. How'd the nursing home get barbecue and iced tea?"

"Mac and I brought it. No sense in their missing out on the fun just because they can't get to the picnic."

"Wonderful. So that's why you were late. Now we'll have to order in a supply of antacid *and* mineral water."

"Yeah, but they'll have fun till then. Besides, what they don't know is that this sauce has a little extra added. If they're going to celebrate, I say let them live it up."

"King Vandergriff, what did Harold put in the barbecue sauce?"

"I'll never tell." He grinned and slipped his arm across the seat to give her a quick hug. "The only thing I hate about this car is its bucket seats. Can't get close enough to my girl."

"I'm not your girl, Vandergriff."

"Yes, you are, for today. For today we're going to call a truce. I'm a regular guy and you're my girl, and we're going to a picnic. How about it, is it a deal?"

"I don't know. I'm not sure I can trust you to be a regular guy."

"If you'll agree to be my girl for the day, I'll be as regular as Old Faithful. Do they have a kissing booth?"

"No, it isn't that kind of celebration."

"Well, who cares?" He stopped at a corner and waited for the traffic to pass. "I don't need a booth, anyway." He leaned across the console and gave her a quick, unexpected kiss. Then he drew back and turned down the street by the police station.

"You're crazy."

"And I'm adorable, successful, logical, and an all-around good fellow. I'm even kind to dogs and old ladies. Look at Minnie Rakestraw. She's two dollars richer because of me."

He slowed the car, pulled into the area marked PARKING, and kissed her again.

"And I suppose you're going to say that you're shy, modest, and unmanipulative," Kaylyn said as she waved to Sergeant Williams, who was grinning broadly from the open doorway of the police station. "No doubt it must be the modest name your family gave you."

"Oh, you don't like being with a king? Okay, then I'll let you in on a deep, dark secret." He got out of the car, walked around to her side, and opened her door. "King isn't my real name. My real name . . ." He leaned closer to her. "My real name is Arthur."

"Arthur?" She began to laugh. "Oh, my gosh. Your name really is Arthur? As in King Arthur and the Knights of the Round Table? It can't be." She thought back on her offhanded comment to Tom earlier in the day.

"One and the same. Don't you think it fits? Play your cards right, darlin', and after the dance I'll show you my sword." He crooked his arm and gave a little bow. "What say you, fair Kaylyn? Shall we go to the fair?"

"Now let's get this straight." Kaylyn licked her lower lip and wiped the spicy red barbecue sauce from her chin. She and King were sitting together at a picnic table, polishing off huge helpings of food. "You have a brother named Jack, who's the architect for your building projects. You have a brother named Joker, who doubles as landscape designer and sales engineer for your jobs. And you have a sister named Diamond, who's the interior decorator. King, Jack, Joker, and Diamond? Your mother must have been a gambler."

"Can't say. She didn't stick around long enough for me to get to know her. My pop named us and dared us to be bums like him. So we worked our tails off to become successful. Now we have Vandergriff, Inc. Classy, huh?"

Classy, yes, she thought. His eyes had turned a smoky blue, and they were filled with a longing that he didn't try to conceal. He combed his fingers through his hair and mussed it, giving it the kind of careless dishevelment that made her want to touch it. His rosy pink shirt hugged his broad shoulders and muscled arms with a softness that gave a gentle touch to his appearance.

Today, in the bright warm sunlight, he seemed more vulnerable, more alone. She reached for his hand without realizing that she'd done so. She could feel the physical differences between them as she surrounded his rough, sunburned fingers with her own softer, tanned ones.

He gazed at her, and the expression in his eyes told her that underneath that hard exterior he wasn't so tough.

"I understand," she said, squeezing his hand. The emotions that he'd exposed were new and confusing. The man inside the sensual body was reaching out to her on another level, opening doors that she hadn't known were closed. "It's rough when you're alone, I know. You just have to believe in yourself. Trust and have faith."

He blinked and looked at her with sudden awareness, as though he'd been in some faraway place and she'd reached him and brought him back. Enormous relief washed across his face. He returned the pressure of her touch. For a moment his gaze rested on her lips, then met hers once more. The wistful longing was replaced with a gentle smile. "The believe-in-yourself part isn't hard, but trust and have faith? That might be a little more difficult."

"Trust and have faith," she insisted.

He lifted her hand to his lips and lightly kissed her fingertips. "I don't think I know about those things, Kaylyn. The only thing I understand is what I can do myself."

His lips were warm and moist, and she felt the

unexpected touch of his tongue as he turned her hand and intimately kissed her palm.

Something changed between them. When he stood and pulled her up beside him, she went without question. Through the crowds they meandered, an acute awareness between them of what was to come. They weren't strangers anymore. Occasionally they separated to move around the people in their paths. Yet with every touch their togetherness grew.

Suddenly Kaylyn laughed, put her arm around his waist, and hugged him, then danced off toward one of the booths with a long line. "Here you are, your highness. I believe you asked about a kissing booth."

King looked at the young men standing sheepishly in line, joking and hitting each other in ill-concealed unease as they waited for their turn to kiss the peaches-and-cream, golden-haired girl inside.

"Well, now," he said. "It looks as if this young lady is going to be pucker-poor before she gets to me. Why don't we give her a break and make some real money for"—he glanced at her sign, which announced that the proceeds were being donated to the Pretty Springs Ballet and Dance Company—"the artistic community."

He pulled a wad of bills from his pocket and stuffed them into the hand of the startled young lady. "Here you are, ma'am." He captured Kaylyn in his arms and kissed her to the applause and amusement of the young boys.

"Hey, how about sharing the wealth?" one of the onlookers called.

"Not a chance, son," King said as he gazed at Kaylyn's flushed face. "This is my own private treasure, and there isn't enough money in the world for you to buy any part of it."

"Don't blame you a bit," Minnie Rakestraw's voice came out of the crowd. "Hello, you two. What about giving Luther and me a push down to the viewing stand? We don't want to miss the tug-of-war, and it's almost time for it to start."

Minnie and Luther were sitting side by side in their wheelchairs under a shady pine tree between the kissing booth and one of the refreshment stands.

"How'd you two get down here?" King asked as he automatically walked behind Luther's chair.

"I had my heart set on a snow cone," Minnie explained, "and Luther hired two of those kids to give me a push. Only trouble was, they heard about the sack race and took off."

" 'Course," Luther said with a grin, "it was a good thing we were here. That little kiss just made Minnie here another dollar."

"All right, you two," King said good-naturedly, "what's this about a romance pool?"

"We just sat down and planned what we'd like to have happen," Minnie said, "and we put a dollar in the pot for each happening. You know"—she blushed—"like moonlight swims, holding hands, kisses. Luther thought you'd kiss her at the VFW hall. Claims it's darker. Old fool. Wishful thinking is what I call it. Got it in his head that *he's* going to get enough better to go back to that VFW hall one more time."

"Well, knowing Luther," Kaylyn said positively, "I wouldn't be at all surprised."

Minnie suddenly dropped her snow cone and looked at it in disgust as it melted in the warm sun. "These damned old dried-up bony sticks. Think I'll just have them all cut off and get me some of them artificial ones. Then I could go to a dance too."

"Now, Minnie." Kaylyn dropped to her knees beside the frail old woman. "You know you're making great progress. A month ago you couldn't even lift that snow cone with either hand."

"That's right," Sandi said as she joined them.

"Hi, Sandi," Kaylyn said. "Where's Mac?"

"He's getting ready for the tug-of-war. He sent me to find out if King wanted to be on the team."

"Only if they let Luther be the anchor," King said with a wink.

"Luther?" Minnie chortled. "What good would he be? He'd get pulled straight into that mud hole, the old fool."

"Shame on you, Minnie," Sandi said. "Look at Luther there. His arthritis was so bad, he couldn't even sit up straight when he got here. Now he's regained the use of both hands, and soon he's going to be bopping around this place on a walker."

"Heaven forbid," Minnie said. "Can't keep him in his room now. He'll get himself thrown out of the home if he gets any friskier."

Kaylyn laughed as she pushed Minnie toward the stands. "Why Luther, what have you been up to that we don't know about?"

"A better question, Katie my love," he said, "is what have *you* been up to over at the springs?" He dropped his voice and added in a conspiratorial whisper that everybody heard, "You know, by yourself, with him. I mean . . . just how well are you getting to know the King here?"

"Bite your tongue, Luther Peavey. I'm just over

there protesting a golf course. What kind of hanky-panky are you suggesting?"

"You might call it hanky-panky, but I call it"—he clutched at his heart and took a dramatic deep breath—"fooling around."

"Maybe we'd better station a chaperon at the nursing home instead of a night nurse, Sandi. I don't know whether or not we can trust these two to behave."

"You'd better not," Luther said. "A few more trips to take the waters and all of you might learn a thing or two."

"Shut up, you old fool," Minnie said. "Don't listen to him, Katie. He's just teasing you. Now, about you and that young man. Well, that's a different thing entirely. Has he held your hand yet?" Minnie asked shyly.

Kaylyn knew she was blushing. Had he held her hand yet? Yes, he had. In fact, there was hardly a part of her that he hadn't held. "I don't think I'm going to tell you, Minnie. You and Luther are too nosy."

"Darn!" Minnie said.

"We're not nosy, personally," Luther said. "We're taking notes for the time when Miss Minnie and I can go dancing and stay out late."

Luther's voice was teasing, but Kaylyn could hear the wistfulness there too. They'd bathed in the springs for an hour that morning. On such days Kaylyn could see a difference in Minnie's grasp. If only they could use the springs on a regular basis, she thought. With a good therapy program and the springs, it was possible that Minnie could regain the use of her left leg and arm. She'd already made remarkable progress.

"You're both going to the dance, Luther," she said. "Everybody who's ambulatory can go. I've arranged special late-night passes for the dance and the fireworks."

They walked down toward the activities area, where Mac joined them. In his short silk running shorts, heavy lumberjack boots, and green socks with a green bandana tied around his forehead, he looked like a refugee from a California beach.

"Are you going to compete, King? I've got a red bandana for you."

"Nope, I'm saving myself for the three-legged race. Kaylyn and I have some serious hopping to do."

They all stayed to watch the tug-of-war. Mac took the forward position on the rope for his team and became the first to tumble into the gooey mud as his side went down to defeat. By the time the children had competed in the tug-of-war and the three-legged race, Mac had found clean clothes and sat in the stands to watch King and Kaylyn compete.

Kaylyn tried to hang back. "Are you sure you want to do this, King? We haven't even practiced, and I happen to know that last year's winners have been working out for the past few days."

King slid his arm around her waist and pulled them tightly together. "We don't need practice, darlin'; we're a natural. You just put your side curves in my side hollows and squeeze up tight. We start off with the outside leg and fly like a butterfly."

The only butterfly Kaylyn could account for was the one hovering just beneath her skin, where she was fitting snugly in King's hollows. How had she ever thought that this kind of race was a laughing matter?

They were making good time halfway into the race when King lurched awkwardly and they hopped madly off-course toward a surrounding patch of pines. Trying desperately to regain his balance, King caught his foot in a tree root, and they both began to roll downhill through the underbrush. In a tangle of arms and legs, they came to a stop in a shallow ravine. The bindings on their legs had come untied. King was flat on his back beneath the thick limbs of a cedar tree, and Kaylyn was lying on top of him.

"King! King, open your eyes. Are you hurt?"

His arms closed around her and he groaned, flexing his body in what felt suspiciously like a caress. "I hurt bad, Kay, darlin'. I need intensive care, beginning with mouth-to-mouth resuscitation."

Now that the anxiety over his being hurt left her mind, she felt a tingle of response sweep over her. "Oh, King," she said hoarsely, giving in to the need to touch him. She nuzzled her cheek against his and hid her face in his neck, feeling the pounding of his pulse in his veins. "You did that on purpose."

"Maybe." His hands slid down her lower back and cupped her bottom. He pressed her tightly against him in a rhythmic motion that moved her up and down his body. "Ah, Kay. You're so beautiful. You belong here, in the woods, with wildflowers in your hair. The animals will all come to bring you gifts and you'll be their queen."

"The queen and her king." She drew back, resting her weight fully on him, feeling the sweet pain of her own body's need. Her eyes were half closed, her lips parted, her breath coming in short, hot pants.

"We lost the race," she whispered. "What will Minnie and Luther think about our disappearance?"

"I don't know about Minnie," King mumbled, "but I'll bet Luther will understand. Oh, lady." He rubbed against her. "I don't suppose we could spend the rest of the day right here, could we?"

He pulled the top of her sundress down, freeing one breast, then moved her body up along his so his lips could find her nipple.

"What if somebody comes by?" Her voice was thick and groggy. She could hear the obvious desire in every word. "Oh, King."

He planted little kisses around her golden brown breast, and up her neck, and reclaimed her lips with an unmistakable urgency. One hand cupped her breast while the other hand gathered up her skirt, his fingers inching beneath it to her bare skin.

Kaylyn was caught up in a torrent of sensation she couldn't hold back. She was pressing herself intimately against him, returning his kisses with rough, urgent ones of her own as her body cried out for the touch of his naked skin against hers.

"Hey, King! Kaylyn, where are you?"

The sound of their names being called finally sank in, and she pulled away from King, forcing back the flood of desire in which she had been swept up.

"Someone is coming, King."

"Damn!" He touched her bare breast once more, then reluctantly recovered it. He rolled her away and sat up. "Whee." He took a deep breath. "I hope that's Mac. I don't think either one of us is in any shape to face someone we don't know." He stood up and openly adjusted his jeans, then held out his hand and pulled her to her feet. "You'd better walk in front of me—and walk very slow."

Her already flushed face turned even redder. "King, I . . . I . . ."

"King, where are you? It's me, Mac, your friendly foreman." Mac spotted King and Kaylyn and came to an abrupt stop, a smile hovering at the corners of his lips.

"You mean, my former foreman," King said. "You're fired!"

"Then call me the advance scout. If we don't get you back in sight pronto, half these people are going to make up a search party to find you."

They had lost the race, but the applause they received from the onlookers was greater than that received by the winners. King had the presence of mind to rub his head, explaining that their fall had temporarily rendered him unconscious. The only dissenting remark came from Luther Peavey, who rolled his eyes and gave a dramatic "Hmph!"

Six

The rest of the day passed in a whirl. Kaylyn no longer tried to resist King's attention. Inviting him to the celebration had been based on two expectations: one, that he'd meet the residents and see how important the springs were to their well-being; and two, that the residents would see him for the commercial entrepreneur he was.

He met the residents, maybe not all of the twelve hundred and fifty official residents of Pretty Springs, but many of them, and he fit right in. They didn't see him as a greedy entrepreneur. And the nursing-home residents liked him almost as much as she did. Nothing had worked out as she'd planned.

Holding hands, they listened to the speeches and ate hot dogs and sweet red watermelon, the juice of which ran down King's chin. They danced for hours in the moonlight on the street, made slick by a generous application of cornmeal. By the time they found a spot on the grass to watch the fireworks,

Kaylyn had given up all pretense at being proper. She sat between his legs with her back against his chest, clasping the arms folded beneath her breasts.

On signal from the fire chief, the city engineer doused the streetlights on the square, and the night went black. When the first spray of color hit the sky, Kaylyn caught her breath and let out a little gasp of pleasure.

"Isn't it beautiful?"

"Not as beautiful as you," King whispered, nuzzling her ear in the darkness.

"Oh, King, stop it. After today it won't be just the nursing-home residents who will be planning our wedding. . . ." Her voice trailed off. "I mean . . . well, you know how small towns are. They'll expect you to—"

Another burst of color mushroomed in the sky. "To what? Make an honest woman out of you?" He waited for the light to die down so that he could slip his fingers beneath her arm, capture her breast, and expose it for a quick kiss before the next flash of light.

"Well, no, not immediately," she said. "But you've staked your claim, and in Pretty Springs that normally means that we would get married." She adjusted the top of her sundress and tried to find a position that didn't allow him such freedom. It didn't work. The finding of the position only made her more aware of the body pressed intimately against her.

"And you don't think that I'm the marrying kind, do you?" he asked.

"Obviously not. After all, you're what—thirty-four, thirty-five? And you've managed to . . ." She sat up straight and looked back at the man who was melting her body into a mass of churning lava. "You're not married, are you?"

He turned her back into the circle of his arms. "I'm thirty-four and available, very available. I'm what Luther calls ripe for the picking—just like you."

She snuggled against him, unable to control her need to be close to the man. "What did he mean, just like me?"

"Luther has a theory. He thinks you need a man to shower your attention on. He says that you've about run out of causes to crusade for in Pretty Springs. The geriatric set is afraid you'll get bored and move on. They're trying to find you a man so that you'll be satisfied to stay here with them."

"And what makes them think you'd be a prime candidate?"

"Because we're good together, Kaylyn Smith. You know it and I know it. We just haven't proved it yet."

Around them the oohs and ahhhs signaled the grand finale of the display, and slivers of brilliant-colored fire danced across the sky. Afterward the watchers began a weary trek back to their cars.

He was right, Kaylyn thought as they walked along with the others. He knew it and she knew it. All the way back to his car, her body clamored for proof. She didn't know what to say. His final statement had gone unanswered.

He helped her inside the car and gave her one quick kiss before he hurried to the driver's side and started the engine. Because he'd parked near the exit, they had left long before the rest of the crowd.

"It's okay, darlin'. I know that this is new to you. Minnie had a few instructions for me too. I'm to go slow and not scare you to death. You're inexperienced. Even if you look like Helen of Troy and Cleopatra all rolled up into one, you're not. I'm to court you slowly. But I think I should tell you, the jackpot in the pool is the wedding. It pays twenty-five bucks."

"Wedding?" King was out of his mind, she thought. The fall during the three-legged race had scrambled his brains. He was talking about weddings as if he might even be half serious.

"Yes," he went on calmly, heading the car toward the springs. "The date is set for Christmas, in the chapel at the Pretty Springs Nursing Home. New Year's Eve is second choice, but the money isn't as good."

"How'd they get so much money in the pool?"

"Well, I have to admit that I put in a few bucks myself."

"Where are you going, King?"

"I'm taking you home, darlin'."

"I—I had intended to stay in my trailer tonight."

"Not a chance, Kaylyn Smith. I want you in my arms, and I don't want to see windows filled with observers keeping score."

"I'm not going to sleep with you, King."

"I've already told you that I don't have sleeping in mind."

He drove through the construction site entrance, passed the Lizard, and parked near the blue-and-white trailer. He walked slowly around the car, opened Kaylyn's door, and caught her hand. "Come inside with me, Kaylyn. Let me make love to you. Please? Forget about Luther and Minnie's expectations. I've never thought about getting married. I've never had much faith in the institution. All I know is that I want you, and for me this is a new kind of wanting."

Kaylyn hesitated. She understood what he was saying. She understood too well. When he brought her hand to his mouth and planted a kiss on the delicate skin of her wrist, she felt herself weaken. What was the point of pretending? She wanted him too. Every time she was around him she became a tongue-tied idiot with a body that seemed to be circulating hot water. And when he kissed her, she turned into one of those fireworks they'd just watched that zinged off into space and shattered into a million pieces.

"This is hard for me to say, King. Luther is right. I am inexperienced with men. I've never slept with a man before. I don't know how to . . . oh, King! I'm afraid."

"I'm afraid, too, darlin', afraid that I won't please you. It's never mattered before. It matters now."

Suddenly she was in his arms and they were kissing each other. The night turned into a beautiful, shimmering swirl of emotions that fueled the fire between them. Then they were inside King's trailer, touching, kissing. Her soft skin came against his hair-roughened body, and the explosion of sensation was as stupendous as the grand finale, except they weren't spectators in this explosion. They were the nucleus.

Kaylyn was lying on King's bed, and she couldn't remember how she'd gotten there. She shivered with intense pleasure as King held her against him, finding for the first time just how well men and women were designed to fit together. His hands skimmed her body, touching, memorizing, pressing. His lips followed as if they, too, needed to inventory her for some memory bank that cataloged every millimeter.

At first timidly, then more boldly, she followed his example. She didn't know what was expected of her. Caught up in the maelstrom of passion, she allowed herself to go where her emotions led her. Her hands rimmed his tiny nipples, almost hidden by thick, soft chest hair. She felt them harden and quiver beneath her touch.

Downward her fingers moved. She was lying half beneath King. One of his legs was thrown across her lower body and pressed intimately between her legs. His lips were assaulting her mouth, and his tongue was exciting her with its intrusion. The involuntary flexing of the muscles in his stomach drew her hand on. Down into the heavier, wiry thatch of hair that surrounded . . .

"My goodness! King!"

He gasped. "Dammit, woman, don't do that, or I won't be any good to you." But he'd already begun to move involuntarily against the hand exploring him with such maddening timidity.

"You won't?" With one fingertip she skimmed the length of him.

"If you're going to touch me, woman, then touch me! Don't make little forays across my body and then retreat. You're driving me to the brink of . . ."

"What exactly am I doing?"

"You can't be that innocent." He gasped, jerking her hand away before she'd pushed him too far.

Kaylyn became very still. She'd offended him but didn't know why. He'd been touching her everywhere. And she hadn't known that her actions would affect him so violently. He was still lying over her, breathing raggedly.

"I'm sorry," she managed to say huskily.

"Darlin' Kaylyn, you haven't done anything wrong. I think we'd better stop and talk for a second. I never thought to ask, but you are protected?"

"Protected? Oh!" She blushed as she realized the meaning of his question. "No. I didn't think . . ."

He groaned.

"I'm sorry, King. I've never . . ."

"Don't be sorry, darlin'. I'll take care of everything—always. Just wait one second."

He rolled across the bed, and she heard a drawer open. Even in the dark she was embarrassed. What was he doing? What was she doing? She shouldn't be here, in King's bed. She'd just . . .

"Kaylyn." He rolled back across the bed, finding her now rigid body. "It's all right, love. You don't have to be afraid, and you don't have to do anything you don't want to. Just let me hold you."

She resisted for a moment, then let him pull her back into his arms. They lay together for a time, listening to the sound of the springs through an open window. Little by little Kaylyn felt her body begin to tingle as if it were awakening. When he moved his hand and lifted her chin, turning her face toward his, she parted her lips and welcomed his kiss.

"Ah, Kaylyn, you are incredible." For the next few minutes he touched her body and described every spot as though he'd been starved and she was rejuvenating his soul. His fingers worked their way between her legs, sending shock waves to the soles of her feet and the top of her skull. She felt the warm moisture of her body welcome his intrusion, and the involuntary contractions of the muscles within went out of control.

Now all thought of refusal vanished. She was on fire. As she felt the great urge to press herself against his fingers she cried out, moaning her needs.

"Oh, Kaylyn, honey. Hold on. I know you want me. I can feel how ready you are. Just a second while I . . ." He pulled away, and the cool air caressed her hot body.

What had she done? she wondered. Had she offended him again with her loss of control?

"King, please . . . please don't stop."

He came back to her and moved over her, pausing for a second as he tried to still the threatening explosion within him. Think of ice, he told himself. Think of those springs, think of the ugliest woman you've ever seen. Desperately he tried to stop the great need his body seemed determined to satisfy.

Dammit, he wanted this to be good for her. No, not just good. He wanted it to be the culmination of all that was right between a man and a woman. Somehow he'd hold back until she was ready. She'd never been with a man before, so he'd have to be careful. Suppose he hurt her? He'd hold back a bit. Suppose . . .

And then the most incredible thing happened. She arched herself up toward him, wrapped her long legs around his back, and pulled him inside her. The thrust was deep and powerful, and she clung to him as sensation ripped through her.

Unable to stop himself, he moved inside her with deep, steady strokes until she began to shudder. "Oh, King. I feel like I'm going to . . . oh! Ahh!" And he answered her with the powerful tremor of his own release.

Sometime later he heard her murmur, "Ah, Matilda . . ."

"Matilda? Not 'darling,' not 'I love you'?"

She smiled in the darkness. There was something so right about the feeling that came from their being joined. They'd become one entity, sharing a beautiful experience, one more wonderful than anything she'd ever dreamed of. She was afraid to move, fearful it would end. How could she have gone twenty-seven years and never known what love was like. Love? Could she have fallen in love with this man? She didn't know. For now she didn't care.

"What about Matilda?" he asked, unwilling to bring the moment to an end.

"I was just thinking that she probably heard me—I mean, us. Do you think she knew what was happening?"

"I think she understood, all right." He kissed her eyelids. "After all, we already know that she's an experienced lady. And she's a pretty smart donkey."

"How can you tell?"

"She likes me." He roused himself, pulling away from her. "Be still, Kaylyn. I'll be right back." He slid over the end of the bed and went into the bathroom. She heard the running of water, and seconds later he was back, lying beside her. She jumped at the unexpectedness of his touch. "What are you doing?"

"I'm bathing you, love."

And he did. The gentleness of his touch was the most incredibly intimate experience of her life.

"I ought to be embarrassed," she whispered. "I can't believe that I'm not."

"Why?"

"There's so much of me," she admitted honestly. "After all, I'm no lithe little thing."

"Every inch of you is perfect, Kaylyn. And every inch of you is mine."

"Really?" Her eyelids were growing heavy as her body seemed to stretch out and relax beneath his sweet touch. "I know that I'm not experienced, but it seems to me that there's pretty much of you too."

He pulled back the spread on one side of the over-size bed, lifted her easily, and deposited her on the silk sheet. "You remember how I told you that one day we'd be totally relaxed in this bed together?"

"Yes."

He slid in beside her, and she allowed him to slip his arm beneath her neck and pull her into his embrace.

"Go to sleep, Kaylyn Smith. I want us to wake up together, still in each other's arms."

"Oh, are we all finished?" She snuggled against him, threading her leg through his with an intimacy that made him catch his breath and force his skittish heart to slow its beat.

"Not on your life, darlin'. We're just resting for a while. I don't want to abuse your body before it's had a chance to adjust."

"Oh, King," she murmured, half asleep. "That's no problem. We have the healing springs. Sooner or later I'm going to make you believe."

Much later King was regretting that he hadn't given those springs a chance. Even in sleep Kaylyn was a nymph. She squirmed closer, rubbing herself against him like a newborn kitten nuzzling its mother. He waited as long as he could. But then he never did have much patience.

For the next few days Kaylyn gave up any attempt to conceal her involvement with King from the community. Her protest was still in evidence, for her tent was still pitched at the springs. But she spent every night in King's bed.

Luther was right about the VFW hall. It was dark, and the dancing was fun. But so was the fine restaurant that King took her to in nearby Atlanta, and the concert in Chastain Park. One night they met Sandi and Mac, Tom, and some other friends at the Waterhole Restaurant. They spent the evening discussing the serious problems of the world amid great joking and laughter. Having friends like that was something new to King. He was beginning to realize how narrow the scope of his life had become.

By the time King accompanied Kaylyn to the Homecoming Services at the Pretty Springs Methodist Church, the foundations for the houses surrounding the golf course had been poured. The tennis courts were being graded and readied for finishing.

"Yes, it was a nice sermon," King said to Homer Langley, the mayor, after the service.

"Matilda hasn't given birth yet?" Esther Hainey asked, inserting herself between King and Kaylyn.

"Not yet," Kaylyn answered. She felt the familiar touch of King's hand on her shoulder as he circled Esther and moved back beside her. "She seems content to stay in her little yard as long as King comes by to check on her daily."

"Really fond of him, isn't she? Donkeys don't usually form that kind of attachment." She aimed a coquettish smile at King. "He must have a special way with all the ladies."

"Only the smart ones, Esther," he said. "And Pretty Springs has a couple of very smart ladies."

Esther beamed as he leaned down and gave her a good-bye kiss on the cheek.

"I'll send the boys over one afternoon to replace that broken section of fence over at the shelter. Then you'll be able to keep any large animals that you collect." He waved as they moved on.

"You know," Kaylyn said to him, "that Esther, Minnie, and half the women in the church are ready to join my protest at the springs just to be near you, don't you?" She leaned against him. Either his hand was resting possessively on her shoulder or gently at the small of her back. He seemed to have a constant need to touch her, to reassure himself that she was there. And she found excuses to stay close to him.

"Too late for them," he said. "I've already been staked out by the most exciting woman in the county. What's all this?"

They had reached the yard adjacent to the church. Wooden sawhorses had been arranged beneath the trees and covered with planks of plywood, making a long table. In no time, white sheets were slung over the table and the women were unpacking huge baskets of food.

"Dinner on the grounds," Kaylyn explained. "Everybody comes from miles around. First there's the church service, then dinner. Afterward there'll be an old-fashioned gospel singing session that will last until late afternoon. This has been going on every summer for over a hundred years."

"Really? These people don't look that old." Despite his humorous remark, King knew that Kaylyn was accomplishing what she'd set out to do. He could see now that Pretty Springs *was* more than just land and potential. It was the people, and their ancestors, and the past. He was slowly being drawn into it all.

A two-year-old darted across the sidewalk and toward the street, but Kaylyn caught him in her arms. She spoke to the smiling child and excused herself for a moment to return him to his very pregnant mother, who was searching the crowd anxiously.

King stood beneath one giant oak tree watching Kaylyn and the child. He thought of Jack, Joker, and Diamond, and how they'd struggled to work their way out of a low-rent housing project by cutting grass and delivering papers until they were old enough to find work at the local fast-food establishments. They'd never even heard of dinner on the grounds, or been to a dance on the town square, or swum in a natural spring. They'd been too busy trying to buy food and keep their father from drinking up their rent money.

Now he drove a Ferrari, Jack had a Mercedes, and Joker wheeled about in the most elaborate van that anybody had ever seen. Only Diamond didn't display her success.

And Kaylyn? As far as King knew, she didn't even have a car. If she'd ever had one, she'd probably given it away to someone who needed it more. She wouldn't measure up in the Vandergriff Blue Book of Success. But, hell, she wouldn't even care. She measured success on a different scale.

"She's something, isn't she?" Tom said, appearing beside King.

"She's more than something," King agreed. "She's probably the most unselfish, giving person I've ever met. She makes me ashamed of my own success."

"She makes us all better people, King. You're no exception. I hate to bring this up. Please don't think I'm being a busybody, but I wanted to make sure you know how very special Kaylyn is."

"I think I know."

"No, this you don't know. Kaylyn's mother was a . . . well, to put it politely, she was a lady of the evening. Kaylyn was a mistake that she didn't take care of soon enough. Kaylyn was placed in a foster home when she was ten. Her mother died six years later. And Kaylyn has spent most of her life trying to right the wrongs that a society imposes on those who can't change their station in life. She's never done anything for herself before you came along."

"Why are telling me this?" King didn't want to hear about Kaylyn. He simply wanted to watch her talking with people, smiling at the children, moving among everyone with ease. Occasionally, she would look up at him. Then, as if reassured, she'd turn back to whomever she was speaking to, only to glance up at him again a minute later. He remembered that first day in the jail cell when he'd thought the flush on her face should come from having spent the night making love with a man. He now knew firsthand the truth of his observations.

"You're the first man Kaylyn's been involved with," Tom said. "I wouldn't want to see her hurt."

"Neither would I."

"Good. She doesn't know how to play games. She's

full of love, and she could never hold back caring for someone. So be sure of what you're doing, King."

King swore silently as Tom walked away. His comments were making King question his own motives.

He reflected on Tom's words as he remembered the young minister's sermon about roots and belonging and faith. He had looked around the church and seen entire families filling pews that were designated by little nameplates dating back fifty years. As he'd stood beside Kaylyn singing the closing hymn, a warm feeling of belonging had crept through him. He wasn't the outsider anymore.

Disturbed by his thoughts, he rejoined Kaylyn. They filled their plates with crisp fried chicken, potato salad, fresh vegetables still warm from their insulated containers, and corn bread dripping with real butter. Thick slabs of chocolate cake and icy sweet tea finished off the monster meal.

Afterward, sitting on a blanket spread beneath the pine trees, they listened to the happy sounds of gospel singing inside the church. Neither of them was inclined to talk. Their silence was warm and comfortable.

If only it could always be like this, Kaylyn thought as she watched a fat yellow wasp circle their blanket and fly off into the hot summer afternoon. If only she could convince King to save the springs and stay in her small town. If only she didn't have this sweet, hurting question inside her, this question that she didn't dare put into words.

"Well, what did you think of the Pretty Springs Founders' Day celebration?" Kaylyn asked.

They were on the way home, pleasantly sleepy and filled with the warmth of their day together.

"I'm impressed," King said. "Do all those folks really come back here every year from wherever they've moved?"

"Yep. The crowd gets bigger every summer. But the format is still the same. Gives you a feeling of stability, doesn't it, to know that some things remain constant?" Even if other things, like the springs, are changing, she couldn't help thinking.

"Oh, I definitely agree. There are some things I'd like to remain the same—like us." He broke the camaraderie between them with a question he hadn't planned to voice. "And then there are other things I'd like changed. Why don't you give up this protest, take down that tent, and move in with me, Kaylyn? I want us to be together—all the time."

Even without looking, he could sense her stiffening.

"Give up on saving Pretty Springs and move in with you? Why should I do that? We're practically living together now."

"That's what I'm saying. Let's be practical. The springs are going to be capped, Kaylyn. I can't do anything about that. But that needn't have anything to do with us. If the trailer isn't large enough, we can get another one. We're good together, you and I. I've never asked a woman to live with me before."

"Live with you." The words weren't a question. Her mind couldn't assimilate the information to compose a question. It seemed to have turned into solid mush that could only echo what it heard.

"Kaylyn, did you hear me?" He parked beside the trailer.

"Yes, I heard you." She opened the door, slid out, and stood looking around the campsite as if she'd never seen it before. "That's like openly consorting with the enemy, isn't it? But, of course, that's what I've been doing. I'm sorry. I guess you're asking for an answer, and I'm not sure how to say what I feel."

King felt his insides twist. She was turning to him, her face sad and filled with regret.

"No. Don't say it, Kaylyn. Don't."

"I'm sorry, King. You don't deserve my refusal. I should have known this would happen. But I didn't. I told you that I had no real experience with men, but of course you found that out soon enough, didn't you?"

He moved toward her, trying desperately to think of a way to call back the words he'd blurted out so thoughtlessly.

"No, please don't kiss me, King. You know that when you touch me I can't refuse you, and now I must."

"I'm sorry, Kaylyn. I didn't mean to say it like that."

"Don't be sorry. You never promised me anything except that I'd sleep in your bed one day. And you were right. I did." She reached into the pocket of her dress and pulled out some money. "Let's see, the way I figure it, my camping bill would be somewhere about fifty dollars. I don't have quite that much here, but I'll get it to you."

"You're leaving?"

"Not the springs, King, just your bed. You still don't understand who I am. By moving in with you, you'd have won. It isn't that I mind losing personally —I do that all the time. But the springs are more important than you and I, and if you don't understand that by now, then you don't understand me. Please, don't touch me, King—ever again."

He watched as she ran past the springs and into her tent. What had happened? he wondered. Only an hour ago they'd been at the church, among friends who had accepted him and made him a part of their simple lives. And like a flash she was gone.

Damn! He sure as hell didn't want to feel responsible for anybody except himself. He hadn't planned on asking a woman to live with him. He hadn't wanted to be a part of Pretty Springs. He'd just wanted Kaylyn. Suddenly he'd lost both her *and* Pretty Springs. He wanted to cry, something he hadn't done in a very long time.

Seven

The next few days passed in a kaleidoscope of pain and confusing emotion. Kaylyn threw herself into her duties at the nursing home with a frenzy of exuberance. She spent time in the church kitchen feeding a dwindling number of the homeless. One by one the men had been adopted into the community and were working for the first time in years. Only two alcoholics were left, and Tom was trying to get them into treatment centers.

After a few attempts at interference from Luther, and offers of advice from Minnie, the residents of the nursing home stopped asking about King. Life settled back to normal, except that the residents began to wish Kaylyn weren't quite so involved with their activities. She'd always kept them too busy to complain before, but now something new was being offered every night. They weren't sure they would survive the pace being set by their recreation director.

"Aren't you overdoing this recreation bit just a

tad?" Sandi asked Kaylyn one day. She was collecting paper cups and wiping spilled ice cream from the activities-room tables. "I mean, I like to churn ice cream as well as the next, and better than most, but ten-o'clock parties are a little late for all of us old folks."

"Is it ten o'clock?" Kaylyn looked at her watch.

"It is. Seriously, Katie, you're about to wear us all out. Now, we go to the springs in the morning, and I've been appointed to ask you not to plan another thing for tomorrow. Okay?"

"I guess I have been overdoing it, haven't I?"

"You have," Sandi said gently. "But we've understood. Most of us have been where you are once or twice, even our jolly geriatrics. But you can't run away from the problem."

"What do you mean, where I am?"

"Come on, Kaylyn Smith. You're heartbroken and lovesick. There isn't a man or woman in Pretty Springs who doesn't know it. The men are threatening to tar-and-feather King Vandergriff and run him out of town."

"No! I mean, this isn't King's fault. He's not responsible. It's me. I'm a dinosaur. I just don't know how to be the kind of woman he wants."

"I'm not so sure," Sandi said mysteriously. "I think you're exactly the kind of woman he wants. I think he just doesn't know what to do about it, but he's working on the problem. Give him time, and some of that faith you have in those mineral springs. Meanwhile you decide what you want."

"What do you mean?"

"I mean that you're in love with the man, and the sooner you realize it, the sooner we're going to get back to normal around here."

"No, I can't be in love with him. The first time I saw him I thought he was a savage, a hawk who hunted his prey. But he isn't. Sandi, he's a tycoon, a self-made yuppie, a smooth ladies' man. He'll finish up this job and take on the next project somewhere on his way to the moon. I'd never fit into his world. I'm just me, one of the little people."

"Then you've thought about keeping him around here?"

"Oh, I've thought about it, but it would never work. There's only one place where we fit together—" Kaylyn stopped, feeling an unwanted blush warm her face.

"Good! I was beginning to think you didn't like sex. I have a suggestion to make, Kaylyn. Why don't you marry him?"

"Me? Marry King Vandergriff? You must be out of your mind. Why on earth would he want to marry me?"

"I can't imagine, unless it's that you two are about perfect for each other—when you're not enemies. Look at what you've accomplished since he came to town. Think about it, friend. Forget about everybody and everything else in the world and think about what you want."

"What do you mean, what I want? Don't stop now, Dr. Arnold, lay it out."

"Well, we love you, Katie, but have you ever considered that you don't have to be all things to all people for us to love you?"

"I don't understand. I simply do things that need doing. There aren't any hidden motives to my actions."

"Maybe there are, a few. We love you, but you need more. We don't want you to turn you into a bitter old prune." Sandi lifted the plastic bag of trash and started toward the door.

"I don't believe I'm hearing this. A bitter old prune?"

"Forget what I said, friend. There's no way you could ever be a prune. I'm just exhausted. I'm taking out this garbage, dropping you at the springs, and heading home. With any luck I might get a late-night telephone call from a certain construction foreman who definitely knows what he wants. Turn out the light and come on."

Kaylyn followed Sandi's directions, her mind whirling with confusion. "Don't make me into a prune and then say forget it, Sandi Arnold. Explain."

"It's that you're almost driven to do things, as though you can never do enough. You ought to go out with a man because you need the man, not because you need him to meet the residents of Pretty Springs or to learn to fit into small-town life, or build a stand, or write a newspaper article. You see what I mean? I guess what I'm saying is that it's time that you admitted you want King for yourself."

Kaylyn fought Sandi's suggestion all the way back to the springs. Was Sandi right? Did she want King for herself? Was that what she was unconsciously doing by remaining at the springs when her protest was an acknowledged lost cause?

After Sandi had dropped her at the springs, she stripped off her clothes and crawled inside her sleeping bag, feeling lonely and confused. All her life she'd tried to do everything she could to make things right for those around her. It made her into a real person. It made her feel good to do good. She gasped. Had she really thought such an unkind thing?

Helping people was right, she told herself. There

weren't enough people in the world who would get involved. If somebody had helped her mother, maybe she wouldn't have lived the kind of life she'd led. Maybe . . . maybe Sandi was right. She'd become so involved with others, she'd managed to close out the hurt in her own life. She'd replaced her loss with the needs of others, and it had become her insulation against anything personal—until King had come along.

Kaylyn turned her face away from the sight of King's trailer. She didn't want to see him. She didn't want to think about him, or feel his arms around her, or his lips on hers. She couldn't deal with that yet. These other feelings were too new and perplexing. With any luck she'd go to sleep quickly before she once more ached for the man who was so near and yet so far away.

Across the springs, King stood at the window staring out at the rocks. More and more he saw them as protective sentries, patrolling the area around Kaylyn Smith. He'd jested about the rocks attacking him, but he was beginning to wonder. Construction around the springs seemed to be crawling along at a snail's pace. They'd had the necessary soil testing done, but the rocks seemed to be shifting constantly beneath the ground, causing equipment problems and breakdowns that were beginning to spook him. That in itself was driving him up the wall.

But more than any problems with the rocks was the constant ache he carried around with him like an inner skin, the ache that pulled his gaze toward that tent and his body toward the springs. He didn't want to admit it, but since he'd stopped swimming in the pool, he seemed tired and sore. And since Kaylyn had left his bed, his temper flared too quickly, and his heart felt as if it had grown too large for the space it occupied.

The phone rang.

"Hey, big bro," Joker's familiar voice came over the line. "How we're doing down there? 'Bout ready for me to come along and set up a sales office to relieve those suckers of their money?"

"Suckers?"

"Those great money moguls who want to retire to our resort and spend their time playing golf and tennis? Our investors are straining at the gills to have a look at their project."

"Well, they can't. Not yet."

"Say, what's wrong, King?"

"Nothing," King snapped. "I'd just prefer that you not call them suckers. This is a nice little community, and I'd like to think that the people we sell to will fit in."

"Well, excuse me. I didn't mean to sound like a con man. Of course, we could ask every buyer to submit to an investigation before we sell to them. There's a problem, isn't there? I know you too well, King Vandergriff. What's wrong?"

"Well, I have run into a small problem down here. There's a woman—"

"Aha, a woman! Now, why didn't I think of that?"

"No, it's not what you're thinking. This woman is special. She's trying to prevent our closing off the mineral springs on the site. It seems the townspeople have been bathing in them for a hundred years. She even chained me to the Lizard and . . ." King's voice trailed off. There was no way he could explain to his younger brother what had happened.

"Lizard? I'm not going to try to understand that one. You've never let a woman slow you down before. Just romance the broad. You know women don't resist the King."

"This one does," King admitted with a wrench in his gut and a pain in his voice that his brother couldn't miss.

"Well, I'm sure you'll come up with something, and soon," Joker said. "The advertising program is under way, and I'll be down in about three weeks to get things rolling. By the way, guess who called about moving in—Tommy Temple."

"Tommy Temple the quarterback? You're joking."

"Not this time, King. Wouldn't it be great if we could get a couple of big-name jocks to buy in? That would just about cinch our success."

Long after he'd hung up the phone, King paced his trailer. Joker was right, he thought. He'd come up with something, he had to. In a few weeks memberships in the Golf and Tennis Club would go on sale, and the houses would be open for examination. And the time was approaching when he'd have to fill in and close up the springs. He opened the refrigerator to see if Harold had left him anything to snack on. No such luck. The only thing he found was a bottle of mineral water from the springs.

"Why not?" He unscrewed the lid and took a long swig. "Hell. It still tastes like dirty seawater."

King was almost back to his trailer the next day when he heard the voices—a man's and a woman's.

They were in the springs. He glanced toward Kaylyn's tent—empty. Well, he'd throw them out right now. The townspeople might as well understand that the springs were off-limits now. He broke into a run, then stopped when the woman spoke again.

"Put your knees on either side of my body and work yourself up and down." The voice was Kaylyn's, intimate and seductive.

"Oh, my." The man groaned. "I didn't realize I would be so stiff. You're just what I've been needing, Kaylyn."

Kaylyn and some bozo were in his springs together? King saw red. He saw white and blue, too, and a full chorus of the "Star-Spangled Banner" was blaring in his head as he catapulted over the rocks and came to a stop at the rocky ledge bordering the pool.

"Kaylyn Smith, what the hell do you think you're doing?"

Kaylyn looked up, her eyes wide with shock, and loosened her grip on the elderly white-haired man she'd been balancing in the water. The man, looking for all the world like Stan Laurel, slid slowly under the water.

"Now look what you made me do!" Kaylyn said angrily. "Mr. Reeves can't swim."

She dived under water. King slung his Stetson over his shoulder and jumped in after her, just as she lifted the old man to the surface. He glanced at King, nodded, and extended one gnarled hand. "Good morning, I'm Walter Reeves. You must be the generous man Ms. Smith told me about."

Now it was King's turn to look like Stan Laurel. He shook the man's hand. "Well, I don't know about that. I'm King Vandergriff. Are you all right?"

"Yes. I knew she'd get me. You can trust Kaylyn. I just held my nose and looked around. Interesting place down there. We don't have anything like these springs in Montana; certainly nothing that gets these arthritic old bones going like I hear these waters do. And to believe that you allow us to bathe in them free! You're a real Good Samaritan, young man."

Kaylyn hadn't said a word. King gazed remorsefully at her, prepared to receive a scathing tongue-lashing. What he got was an attempt at suppressed laughter. The attempt was unsuccessful. Kaylyn began to giggle in spite of herself. The giggle turned into a full belly laugh that was contagious. Suddenly all three of them were laughing wildly.

Gasping for breath, Kaylyn turned to King and asked, "What on earth did you think we were doing, Good Samaritan?"

King looked sheepish. "Don't ask." He glanced down at his feet, still under water. "I'm just glad that these boots are made from alligators."

"Your boots! You've probably ruined them," she exclaimed in dismay.

"Not to worry, darlin'. This successful entrepeneur type will just buy some more. Since I'm already in over my head, what can I do to help?"

"You're serious?" Kaylyn had forgotten Mr. Reeves. From the moment King had joined in on the laughter, the world had brightened. Foolish? Yes, but the feeling inside her had simply burst loose, like the water falling over the rocks behind her. She felt good all over.

"I never make idle offers," King said seriously. "You know me batter than that, Ms. Smith. Always direct and to the point. Let's do it!"

He leaned down in the water and removed the alligator-skin boots and red socks one at a time and flung them toward Kaylyn's tent. His shirt and jeans followed. If Walter Reeves was surprised by King's red briefs, he didn't show it.

Kaylyn, however, was temporarily speechless. She could only stare in appreciation at the wavering image of slim, muscular legs and massive thighs. She'd missed those legs and those outrageous briefs. She'd missed King and the good feelings that washed over her when he was nearby. She'd missed their doing things together.

"Now," he said, breaking into her thoughts with a knowing smile, "I believe you had prescribed some kind of up-and-down motion for stiff bodies. Do let me help. This exercise sounds like a move I'd find very helpful for a problem I've had lately."

"Oh?" She refused to look at him as she manipulated Walter's knees back and forth. "I thought you knew all the moves."

"It isn't a matter of knowledge," King said, using his chest as an anchor against Walter's back as he supported the man in the water. "It's a matter of not being able to get the necessary kind of medical treatment in my time of need. These springs do marvelous things," he confided to the still grinning Mr. Reeves. "Has she told you about the theory that they will restore certain power to men who are—"

"King! Lift Walter a bit higher while I manipulate his limbs. Walter, forget King and concentrate on moving your body."

"Good idea, Walter. You'd better do as she says. This woman is a personal friend of the rocks that guard these springs. If you cross her, they get even.

Believe me, I know. They've been on my case for the last week."

Kaylyn looked at King seriously over Walter Reeves's head. "Is something wrong, King?"

"Not anymore, darlin'. Not anymore."

"You mean that Luther was as crippled as Walter Reeves when you started bringing him here?" King asked that night. Reluctantly he had gone to work after Kaylyn had returned to the nursing home earlier in the day. The hours had seemed to crawl by until she finally came back long after dark. He had pulled on a pair of black swimming trunks and strolled casually over to the springs, announcing his plan to take a late-night swim. Without an invitation, Kaylyn, wearing a black tank suit, soon joined him.

After a brisk swim King was sitting on the rocks across the springs from Kaylyn, wishing they were side by side. This was the first time they'd been alone together since the Church Homecoming and Dinner on the grounds, and he was afraid to try to return to their former relationship too quickly. Even a simple swim was a gamble.

"Yes," she answered, "and you can see how far he's come. The springs, the exercises . . . I can't explain the healing process, I just know that the power is there."

"If these springs are as remarkable as you claim, why hasn't the medical world acknowledged them?"

"I'm not sure, King. The Cherokee knew about the healing powers. Back in the 1800s the medical authorities were so convinced of their power that an international conference of physicians was held here. The waters were sent all over the world and endorsed as a medical treatment, but as time passed, other medicines were invented and the springs fell out of fashion, except to the old ones who remembered."

King kicked his feet in the water, watching the ripples in the moonlight. "It seems to me that for medicinal purposes it would be more helpful to arthritis if the water weren't so cold."

"You're right. I've tried my best to think of a way to heat them . . . but they don't belong to me, and I couldn't convince the new owner to cooperate."

"Kaylyn, if I ask you a question, will you give me an honest answer?"

"I'll try."

"If you were able to set up a pool in the nursing home that was heated properly and equipped for therapy and could put these people through the same exercises, wouldn't you get the same results? I mean, isn't it really a matter of the mind believing and the body's being conditioned?"

"Perhaps," she said, trying to be as honest as she could, "but in order to have the same results, we'd have to duplicate the springs' mineral content, and there is no way we can do artificially what nature has done naturally. It's been tried."

"I see." What King really saw was a woman who fervently believed in a cause, a woman whose unwavering faith had been tested and found justified. He was confused and a bit angry. How could he fight her belief in the springs without destroying what was between them?

"Kaylyn, I need to explain about our company.

Vandergriff, Inc., is a small operation that is making its first bid at the big time. We don't own this land alone. We have investors, investors whom we have to please, investors who have put up the money to underwrite the construction costs. Even if I wanted to save your springs, I'm not sure it could be done."

"Can't you give them back their money? I'm sure the Pretty Springs Bank would lend you the money to build your houses."

"Oh, Kay, darlin', you have no conception of what's involved in a project of this size. Even Georgia National Bank wouldn't underwrite the whole project here. The only way it could work is if the springs could be incorporated into the center and somehow be made to pay for themselves. At the moment I can't see a way. But I'll try, darlin', I promise, if you'll give me another chance with you."

"You mean more bartering, more 'me for the springs'?"

"No, these springs have had you long enough. I want you for myself. I don't want to scare you off, Kaylyn, but I want to be honest with you. This is very serious. You see, I'm not sure that I can do anything about the springs, though I'm going to try. I think I may be falling in love with you, Kaylyn. I want to think that nothing is important enough to come between us."

Kaylyn's feelings for King temporarily overwhelmed her, and she could only stare at him with her heart in her eyes. "What did you say?" Her voice was hushed and uncertain. The gurgle of the springs seemed to stop, and there was a thundering silence in her mind.

He took a deep breath and held on to the rough

edges of the rock to keep from vaulting over the springs and taking her in his arms. "I said, Kay, darlin', that once I got over my anger and quit fighting the feelings you arouse in me, I realized that I was falling in love with you. I'm not sure what I should do about it."

"Oh, dear." She stood up and glanced around the hewn-out area in the rocks where she'd been living for the last few weeks. Moonlight had thrown a coat of soft, glittery light across the rocks, turning the streaks of minerals into smears of silver and gold. This was a magic place. She'd always known that. But she'd never felt the magic herself, until tonight. "Oh, King, I'm afraid."

He stood. She watched the water roll off his strong shoulders, making rivulets that ran down his chest to his solid legs. He was some man, some beautiful man, and he'd just told her that he was falling in love with her. Bemused, enchanted, filled with wonder, she held out one hand, as if in protest to the feelings rushing through her. Across the springs, a wince of pain wrinkled King's brow, and she felt his hurt as clearly as if he'd spoken it. She lowered her hand and turned it palm up so that her gesture became a plea of entreaty. And she smiled.

"King?"

He gave a cry of pleasure and came to her. There in the moonlight, on the rocks, he took her in his arms and kissed her. The springs gurgled back to life and plunged musically across the rocks to the pool.

"Thank you, you big, dumb rocks," King said hoarsely. "You finally did something good for me."

"Oh, King. I've missed you so much!" she said, choking. "I didn't know how bad it would be."

He kissed her again and groaned. "Neither did I. Even Harold resigned his job. Said life at the jail was more peaceful."

"I don't know if there is an answer or not, King, but I know that I care about you. You make me feel happy . . ." She struggled for the right words. "Feel happy for *me*. Do you understand?"

"Yes," he said softly. "I think I do." In his wildest dreams he never thought he could ache this badly, desire a woman so passionately, want so much to make her happy.

Kaylyn felt the muscles of his back tremble beneath her hands. She almost stopped breathing as he tightened his hold on her and lifted her up against him. The feel of his arousal set off an answering response within her that she made no attempt to restrain.

"King, I don't think I can stand up much longer. I want you. I want you inside me. I think I'll die if you make me wait."

He didn't. The extra-soft padding of the tent floor became a featherbed as he peeled the swimsuit from her body and laid her back. She watched him as he shimmied out of his own black suit and stood over her like the savage she'd first believed him to be.

"You're a magnificent man, King Vandergriff. When your father named you, he must have known that this moment would come someday. I think you belong here in this place, even more than I."

"I only belong where you are, darlin'."

He had come prepared, and quickly readied himself. Then he knelt over her, sliding himself against the sweet moistness of her desire until he was certain she was as ready as he. Tentatively, gently, he entered her, holding back for fear of hurting her. He felt her open herself to take him in, then she flexed her muscles, tightening herself around him. He lay still and content as the feeling inside him hovered near the point of explosion.

"You know," he whispered as he nuzzled the spot beneath her left ear, "you're right—what you said that first day on the rock. You are honey-colored all over."

"And I'm going to hold you to your bragging," she said, forcing herself to stay still beneath him.

"How's that?"

"You said you were going to kiss every inch of my body."

He started to move inside her, and she gasped as the rocks beneath them seemed to tremble.

"Later," he said with a growl. "Much, much later."

His mouth captured hers, and his tongue dove deep inside. They became one being, as every part of them was transported into a mystical realm of sensation. They gave all of themselves to each other, and even in the splendor of the moment they knew they would never again be the same.

Through the soft hours of the night they lay together and loved again and again. The magic stayed with them, and they left all conscious thought behind as they gave in to the silver-edged dreams that had become their reality. And the spring bubbled to the surface and rolled across rocks that had endured for two hundred thousand years. And in the distance the Lizard kept watch.

King was leaning on one elbow, splaying his fingers across Kaylyn's breast. He loved to look at her. For the last half hour he'd touched her breasts, watching her nipples stiffen and relax. He'd touched her navel and explored the mat of soft golden curls between her legs. She was a spectacular woman. He'd spent most of the night relearning the body he was watching.

"Wake up, darlin'," he whispered, touching his lips to her eyelids.

She opened her eyes shyly. Seeing King's sweet smile glowing down over her was a new experience. "I wasn't asleep."

"Oh, yes, you were. I know you well enough to know that you'd never lie still for what I've been doing if you hadn't been asleep."

"I was dreaming the most marvelous dreams. Why'd you wake me?"

"Because I have to go. I don't want to leave you, but I'm already late for work. Will you be here when I get back?"

His question was more than an inquiry about where she'd be for the day. He was asking her for a verbal commitment that their night had meant the same to her as it had to him. She could feel the tension in his body as he awaited her answer.

"Yes," she said softly. "I'll be here. You have your own work to do, King, and I have mine. I have to make arrangements for prizes for the weekly bingo game at the home, but that shouldn't take long. I'll be back." And she would. Even knowing that his work would hurt something she cared for, she'd return. "Somehow, somewhere, I have faith that we'll find an answer."

"I like your faith, Kay, darlin'. I only hope . . . well,

I'll be back at lunch." He kissed her lightly, then allowed the kiss to deepen as she responded naturally. "I don't think I can wait any longer to see you again."

"Lunch it is," she agreed, reluctant now to loose her arms from around his strong, firm body. "King, this is all new to me, and I don't want to make you late, but would you think me a wanton hussy if I asked you to kiss me once more?"

"Ah! Be a wanton hussy. Who cares if I'm late? I'm the boss, aren't I?"

"Definitely," she said, and gave him complete control. The prizes could wait indefinitely, she decided. The bingo game could always be postponed. The residents would have much more fun reactivating the romance pool. This was her time—and King Vandergriff was her man. She might just take out an ad in the *Pretty Springs Gazette*: "Do-gooder is done good by Good Samaritan." She giggled. At least it started out as a giggle. What it changed to was something much more sensual and satisfying.

If the springs seemed to churn more loudly than usual, the workers beyond the rocks just wrote it off to pressure from deep within the earth.

Eight

"Sorry, bro," Joker's familiar bearlike growl came over the phone line, "but the investors will think you've split your gourd."

"Maybe I have," King said in a soft but determined voice, "but it could work."

"Yeah, and frogs could take up clogging and be on the Grand Ole Opry. Look at this sensibly. Our little project is supposed to bring in folks with big bucks, folks that play tennis and golf and take jaunts out to Las Vegas and an occasional trip to Europe. That doesn't mix with little old men and women with medical problems."

"You don't think they might be philanthropic with some of those bucks? These local people won't bother the residents. All we have to do is enclose the springs in a building and allow Kaylyn to oversee the project. I've been considering offering her a job, anyway. Think of the great public relations."

"Think of the money we'll lose if our investors hate your little scheme and pull out."

"Talk to them, Joker. This is really important—to me."

"No way, King. You're the smooth-talking businessman. I just deal with the ordinary Joe who has money to blow on houses, and dreams of being part of the establishment. If you want our moneyed backers sold, you'll have to do it. I'm not saying don't try it, but I am saying be sure you know why you're taking the risk. Remember, your family has come a long way—the hard way."

"But . . ." King thought of Kaylyn and the time they'd spent in her tent at lunch. He thought of their plans for him to pick her up after the bingo game and return to his trailer. He hadn't promised her that he'd find a solution to the destruction of the springs, but he'd silently vowed as he held her that he was going to try. He knew that she trusted him. He didn't want to let her down. Still, there were others to consider.

Joker had hit the nail on the head. He would be taking a risk. Did he have the right to take such a chance with a scheme that could ruin the others, for the sake of a woman's faith in some healing springs? They'd worked for so long to reach this point, the three of them. And Diamond—this would be his sister's first real chance to show her decorating skills. He felt the questions bounce off him like the rain had bounced off his trailer that first night with Kaylyn.

Kaylyn. All he had to do was say her name and all his worries faded away into nothing. The springs didn't have anything to do with his problem. He wasn't sure he believed in their power, anyway. All of his indecision was for her, because of her quiet faith in the springs—and because she cared. And suddenly he understood that he cared too. He cared very much for the woman, and he'd do whatever it took to be a part of her life.

"I know you won't understand, Joker, but it's for Kaylyn, and for Harold, Luther, and Minnie. I'm not sure that I understand it myself, but they've taken me into their town and into their lives and made me feel like I'm one of them. For the first time in my life I belong someplace. I never realized before how much I wanted to belong."

"Sounds like this is some woman," Joker said quietly.

"She is. But it isn't just her. It's the others too. Why, you wouldn't have believed the Founders' Day Picnic. And . . ." His voice trailed off as he realized the next statement he was about to, but didn't, make: *Someday I want Kaylyn and I to bring our children to the Founders' Day Picnic and dinner on the grounds at the church.*

"Sounds like the great man has gone and let a little Georgia girl lasso and hog-tie him." Joker didn't speak again for a moment, then added seriously, "I'm glad for you, King. Don't let me blow it for you. Do whatever you think best, we'll stand behind you. It's always been the Vandergriffs against the world, and I'm sure that Diamond would love having another woman around to keep us in our place."

"Thanks, Joker. I know it doesn't make any sense, but I have to do it. I'll fly up to Nashville tonight."

• • •

At first the investors turned King down. Then they agreed to give the Vandergriffs an opportunity to come up with a workable solution.

For the next two weeks King worked with the investors. Joker advertised in major newspapers. Tommy Temple contacted teams and lined up other professional athletes who wanted living quarters in the development.

After a little prodding with the threat of bad publicity from Tom Brolin as editor of the *Pretty Springs Gazette*, the investors agreed to save the springs. The only problem was that they refused to increase their money allotment for the clubhouse. A spa and medical center for rehabilitation work would require a much larger financial commitment, and they were satisfied with the original plan. If King could do it under the present budget and the residents were willing to pay the necessary fees to change the plans, the investors would agree. Otherwise, no soap.

Temporarily defeated, King flew back to Atlanta and drove to the springs to face Kaylyn with his failure. His plan had been wonderful. At least he'd saved the springs, but he still had no idea how he could keep them open for Kaylyn's patients.

King stepped off the plane at Hartsfield International Airport a few minutes after midnight. A forty-minute drive took him to the springs and his trailer. All he wanted was to stride across those rocks and crawl inside Kaylyn's tent. But he held back. He was more tired than he realized. He needed time to find the words to explain what he'd done, so that she wouldn't think he'd let her down.

After unlocking the door to his trailer and stepping inside, he noticed that the air conditioner was running. He stood in the darkness for a moment, aware of an unmistakable sense of completeness. The strong aura of Kaylyn's presence surrounded him. He walked across the living room and down the hallway. Kaylyn was sleeping in his bed, one arm curled behind her head, looking like a fairy-tale princess waiting for her prince to come. He hadn't expected to find her here. His heart swelled in his chest. The tired feeling of defeat slowly ebbed as he shed his clothes and crawled in beside her.

"How'd it go, sport?" She curled naturally into his arms and sighed in contentment as he held her close. She wasn't wearing any clothes. The feel of her skin against his body felt right.

"It was a drag." He kissed her, closing off the questions he didn't want to hear, and the answers he didn't want to give. "I've missed you."

"I've missed you, too, you big galoot. I thought you'd never get back. It's only been two weeks, and it feels like two years."

"I'll never do that again," he said, sliding his hand down to cup her buttocks. "God, Kaylyn, it seems like forever since I've held you like this. Never again."

"Never is a long time, King. Don't make promises you can't keep." She rubbed her face against his chin, reveling in the feel of the rough stubble of beard against her skin.

"I like holding you," he murmured, "feeling your body against mine, smelling that crisp, clean fragrance of the spring water in your hair. You're the loveliest human being I've ever known, Kaylyn Smith, and the most beautiful."

"I'm no such thing," she protested. "Let me check your nose." She pulled her hand away from the shoulder she'd been clinging to and found his nose in the darkness. With light, feathery sweeps she ran her fingers up and down it, and across the lip beneath. "Well, it seems all right so far."

"What seems all right?" He caught her fingers and held them against the strong pulse beat in his neck.

"Your nose. It hasn't started to grow, so you're not turning into Pinocchio—yet. No more exaggerations. I couldn't stand you with a great, long proboscis. It would interfere with my doing this." She brushed her lips against the tip of his nose and worked downward across his cheek, allowing her tongue to taste him as she reached his lips.

The heat of their contact drenched any thought of the slow, gentle loving that King had envisioned. He moaned and whispered hoarsely, "I want you, Kay. I need you. I've thought about this moment every second of the time I was away. I was afraid. . . ."

"Don't be afraid, King. I'm here. And I want you too."

"You feel so good," he whispered to her a short time later. "I feel so good. I'll never get enough of you."

She felt him begin to stiffen again. Only a slight movement but it was there, and her body was giving its own signals of response as her muscles contracted in answer.

"Oh, Kaylyn. I hope I didn't hurt you just now. I guess I was an insensitive devil rushing into you like that, but I couldn't hold back. This time we'll take it slow and easy. I want it to be good for you."

"King, if it gets any better, I may dissolve into a pool of heat and disintegrate before your very eyes."

With slow, gentle motions he began to move inside her again. Then suddenly he raised up, his body stiffening. "Wait! Dammit, Kaylyn. Stop!"

"Why? What's wrong, King?"

"My darlin' love," he whispered in great disgust, "I forgot. I wanted you so bad that I never even thought. I didn't protect you."

"It's all right, King. While you were gone, I took care of that myself. Just in case, you understand. I knew that you didn't need to worry about my getting . . . I mean, you and I know what it's like not to have both parents, and I didn't want us to do that to a helpless child. I mean . . . well, you know."

"You took care of the problem?" He should have been pleased. Why wasn't he? The thought of Kaylyn being pregnant, carrying his child, was something he hadn't contemplated until he heard that she'd chosen not to do it. There was a queer, twisting ache inside him that he couldn't identify.

She lay still and silent beneath him, staring at up him. "What's wrong, King? Did I do something wrong?"

"No, darling," he muttered, "of course not. I'm just surprised. I mean, I know that it must have been embarrassing for you . . . I mean, since you'd never done that kind of thing before, have you?"

"That should have been fairly obvious, King." A coldness was boring through her. He wasn't pleased. She'd taken too much for granted. Maybe a woman wasn't supposed to admit that she wanted a man and expected him to make love to her. Maybe only the women King had been involved with in the past would have done such a thing. She'd become just like them, and now he was disappointed.

He felt her drawing away from him and panicked. "Kay, my love"—he kissed her eyelids—"thank you." His lips moved down to her nose and her upper lip.

"Are you sure?"

"I'm sure. Knowing that you wanted this—and us—makes me so very happy." He found one breast and lifted it to meet his lips. "Please, I never want to cause you pain. I'm sorry if my poor choice of words has distressed you." He felt her shift her weight so that he was halfway inside her and throbbing with ecstasy. "I've never lo— cared before."

She made a low sound of deep emotion. "You're driving me crazy, King. Inside me, all of you, don't hold back. Please, don't tease me anymore. This time I won the betting pool and the prize is . . . ahhh!"

"Sweetheart, it's Joker who's the tease, not me. And I think that I can't possibly . . . I mean, I don't want to hurt you. It's been two weeks." Even in the heat of his passion King had forced himself to hold back, pulling out instead of entering her warm, tight body, which seemed determined to hold on. He didn't want to hurt her.

"Hellfire, King Vandergriff. In case you haven't noticed, I'm a big girl." She gasped in pleasure. "And I want you, all of you—now."

She pulled her legs up, folded them around his waist, and dug her heels into his back in a sudden motion that thrust him deep inside her. He felt all the heat in the universe converge as they came together. His release was a centrifuge of heat that spun them both off into a kaleidoscope of pure delight.

"Oh, King, does it just get better and better?" She was completely drained. She couldn't have moved if she'd wanted to. But she didn't. She just wanted to lie there and experience the gentle sensation of total satisfaction, satisfaction brought to her by the man still holding her. Sleep was claiming her, shy and warm like a baby's soft blanket. She had never been so happy.

"Oh, yes, my darling Katie," he murmured. "Together we just get better and better." He kissed her neck and felt his own eyelids grow heavy. "You sound like you looked that first day in the sun, like a woman truly loved by a man who's finally found what love really means."

"There, you did it again, called me Katie. You've never done that before. Why?"

"I don't know. I guess it was everyone else's name for you. It was warm and gentle, and it put me too close to you."

"And now?"

"I don't think I could get any closer, darlin', and I'm damn sure nobody else will."

"You are?" She liked the way his arm felt under her neck, his chest beneath her face. She loved everything about this man. She knew her mind was becoming fuzzy. She wasn't sure whether she was whispering out loud or merely telling herself when she said, "I'm sorry, I can't talk anymore. I'm very, very sleepy. I love you, King Vandergriff."

His, "I love you, too," became a part of her dream, as did the hand that held her breast throughout the night.

• • •

The knock on his trailer door seemed to be a muffled echo of the pounding of his heart as King tried to stop the noise from disturbing his dream.

"Go away!" He was holding Kaylyn and didn't want to wake up and find it was all a dream.

"Not a chance, boss," Mac answered. "You'd better get out here and see about this donkey."

"Matilda?" Kaylyn said sleepily.

He wasn't dreaming. Kaylyn was in his bed; he was holding her breast, and there was an earth-shattering knock jarring the trailer.

"Ah, hell!" He slid out of the bed and strode toward the door.

"King!" Kaylyn called in a panic. "Your robe!"

"Oh." He whirled around and grabbed a black velour robe hanging on the back of the door, jerked it open and pulled the robe on as he strode down the hall.

"What the hell's going on, Mac?" he asked as he opened the trailer door.

"It's that donkey. I think she's having her colt or kid, or whatever donkeys have."

"So? Why wake me? I'm no veterinarian."

"It's where she's having it that I'm disturbing you about."

"And where is that?"

"Somebody didn't fasten the gate tight, I guess, and she's right in the middle of the equipment area, under that big tractor with the oversize pan. We can't budge her, and we can't move the machine without running over her. And we can't find Kaylyn anywhere to help us get her back into her pen."

"Is she all right?" Kaylyn asked. She was rubbing

the sleep from her eyes as she walked over to stand beside King, wrapping a matching velour robe around her without a thought. "Good morning, Mac."

"Uh . . . good morning, Katie. Sorry to . . . uh, disturb you, but I don't know nothing 'bout birthing no donkey babies."

Kaylyn smiled. She didn't know if the news about Matilda made her happier, or if her happiness was so great that she would have grinned at the announcement that the police station was on fire.

"Well, call the vet," King said. He slid his arm around Kaylyn and pulled her close. He no longer cared if the men knew what was happening. He wanted to touch Kaylyn, and it didn't matter whether or not Mac understood.

"Sure, boss. What about the machinery?"

"We wait."

"And the men?"

"Send out for coffee. Tell them they're on maternity break until Matilda's baby comes. Anything else?"

"No, I guess not." Mac glanced at Kaylyn, smiled, and backed slowly down the steps and away.

"Now"—King closed the door and turned back to Kaylyn—"where were we? Good morning, darlin'." He bent his head and kissed her.

"Hadn't we ought to get dressed and give Matilda our moral support?" She felt the belt to her robe fall open as he brought their bodies together again.

"Not just yet."

"But don't you think your crew is going to wonder about us?"

"I suppose," he said reluctantly, staring at her with eyes filled with passion. "All right. We'll dress and check on our foster child."

"Then you'd better stop what you're doing quick," she said hoarsely. "It feels too good."

"Tell me about it." His hands had worked their way down her spine to her hips and were holding her tightly against his hardness.

"King," she warned, "we'd better stop. Harold will be here soon. He's going to do your laundry."

"Harold?"

"Yes, you remember Harold, our old friend from the drunk tank." King was sliding himself back and forth between her legs, setting off exquisite spasms of pleasure in her body.

"Yes." His breath was coming fast, and he could hear Kaylyn gasping softly. "Has he stayed sober while I was gone?"

"Oh, yes. In fact, he's even found himself a real job over at the nursing home. He's going to be one of the night orderlies."

"Harold?"

"You ought to see him in his white uniform." She closed her eyes at the ecstasy he was creating in her. "Oh, King! Maybe . . . maybe if we hurry."

They did.

Matilda didn't.

By the time the tiny mule was finally delivered, half the day had been wasted and the men were openly shaking their heads in amazement over their boss's new concern for causes and protestors. Kaylyn had missed arts and crafts at the home, and most of the special afternoon movie being shown on the new VCR that had been anonymously donated to the nursing home the day before, but she managed to put in a few hours' work planning for upcoming activities and events.

It was early evening before Kaylyn returned to her campsite. There was no sign of King at the trailer. Harold finished the laundry and left for the nursing home, and Kaylyn walked around the campsite feeling lonely and a little scared. Where was King? Had he gone away again? If so, why hadn't he mentioned it? Finally she gave up and crawled into her tent. It had been one thing to sleep in his bed when he'd been in Nashville trying to save her springs, but now she felt very strange about the relationship she'd allowed herself to fall into.

Tonight the sound of the springs didn't bring the comfort she'd always felt. She realized that King had carefully avoided any mention of a trip or what he was doing. Maybe she'd misunderstood. No, she couldn't be wrong about what they felt about each other. Nobody could misunderstand that. Unless she'd been wrong. Maybe everybody had those same sensations. Maybe she was only another notch on King's alligator belt. Maybe . . .

Kaylyn tossed miserably for almost an hour before she drifted off into a troubled sleep.

It was late when King was forced to admit defeat, board a plane for the short flight back to Atlanta, and return to the springs. His last attempt to convince the backers to increase their investment in order to build the spa and medical complex met with sincere regret and a firm rejection. He didn't know how he'd explain the truth to Kaylyn, but he couldn't stay away from her.

He crawled into her tent and slid into the sleeping bag with her. He put his arm beneath her neck and felt her turn to him with a deep sigh of pleasure. She didn't wake, and he didn't rouse her. For now he was content just to hold her and know the joy of being close to her. He still had to tell her that he hadn't been able to find a way to open up the springs to the locals. But he hadn't given up. There was always tomorrow.

And tomorrow began with the morning.

King fell asleep planning just how he intended to wake Ms. Kaylyn Smith—very, very early.

Nine

"So that's it, Kaylyn. I managed to save the springs, but keeping them open to the public . . . well, the powers that be just aren't going to let it happen."

"I see."

They were sitting at the small Formica table in King's kitchen. Their knees almost touching, he was holding her hands in his. Kaylyn noticed the patches of light hair growing on his fingers. This hair was more wiry than the hair on his chest and legs, she thought idly as her mind took in what he was saying.

"I'm sorry, Kaylyn. I tried. Truly I did. But you have to understand that no matter how much we'd like to change them, there are some things that have to be."

"My mind understands," she said in a voice strained with disappointment, "but my heart says that if you really wanted to, you would pick up one of my protest signs and tell them all to go take a flying leap off the Lizard."

"I could, but it isn't just me—there are too many other things involved. You see that, don't you?"

"No." She drew her hands away and looked up, squinting with pain at the possibility that he might be right. "No, I don't."

"Please, Kaylyn, I care about you. Don't let your attachment to the springs destroy our relationship. I can finish up here and we'll take a trip, get to know each other. I don't want to lose you, darlin'. We're too good together."

She looked out at the springs. She didn't trust herself to speak. She'd wanted King, and she'd given herself to him. And he was right, they were "good" together. But a relationship? No, they couldn't have a relationship built on giving up. "I'm sorry, King. I know you tried. And I'm not turning my back on you. I'm turning my back on a relationship. Somehow there must be a way for us and the springs. I'll just have to find it."

She stood up, and King felt a terrible foreboding. She was leaving. What they'd shared wasn't important to her. He hadn't known what to expect when he'd told her the sad truth. But he'd been foolish enough to believe that what they shared was strong enough to weather the loss of the springs. Hell, he didn't want just a relationship. He wanted Kaylyn—now, tomorrow, and forever. But he'd been afraid that she wouldn't accept him without the springs.

Kaylyn looked at him. Lord, he was one handsome man. She could tell that he was shaken. Conflicting feelings tumbled through her. She felt as though she were being split in two. Half of her was like ice, while the other half wanted to reach out and fold herself into his arms and stay warm and protected.

She didn't know how to separate what she wanted from what she had to be. What she wanted was King, but she had a commitment to her patients, her friends, her town. King had a commitment, too, to his family and his investors. One side of her had to lose. She didn't know if she could love him when so many people were going to be hurt.

As though he could sense the rip inside her, in the very essence of her, King's expression became bittersweet and resigned. He loved her. Confusion, hurt, and anger were warring inside him. He'd never loved anyone, other than his brothers and his sister. He didn't know what to do when that love threatened the only reality in his life. He'd betrayed her faith and become diminished in her eyes. King was shaken to the core. He couldn't have it all.

There was no mathematical formula to guide him now. This action plus that action didn't produce the desired result. He was floundering badly. There'd been many failures in his life. He'd learned to deal with them, not by acceptance but by diverting his energy to another problem. Why couldn't Kaylyn see that there came a time when a person failed and there was nothing he could do?

"I'm sorry, King. I need to think. We both need time to think." She saw the anguish in his eyes. It was the final wrench that tore her heart apart. Whirling, she fled. She ran across the rocks and down the path to the Lizard. Leaning her head against the rock, she wept in uncontrolled abandon.

"Damn you, King!" She hadn't cried for herself in years, not since the door had closed behind her at her first foster home. She'd sworn then that nothing and nobody would ever hurt her again. She had never shed another tear over her own pain—until now. The Lizard was cold and hard. She felt the rough edges of the rock dig into her forehead and welcomed the pain. "Damn all the men with money. Damn dreams that cause such misery and pain."

She let herself cry until there were no more tears. Finally she slid to the ground and leaned against the big stone, seeking some comfort from its solid presence. She closed her eyes. The summer sun fell over her with a deep, penetrating heat.

What was she going to do? The city fathers didn't seem to find the loss of the springs a handicap to the town. They'd rather have the influx of new people and new money. With that money they could improve the schools, build new roads, and benefit more people than she'd ever reach with her little plans. Sacrifice the needs of a few for the needs of many—that was the modern way. Maybe they were right. Other than her nursing-home residents, nobody seemed to care.

"Kaylyn?" Mac had come up behind her and stood over her, an odd expression of reluctance on his face. He hesitated, then said, "King sent me to check on you."

"I'm fine, Mac," she said wearily as she pushed herself up to her feet. "Would you give me a lift into town?"

"Sure. I'll get my Jeep."

Mac didn't question her on the way into town. He wanted to speak. Kaylyn could tell that he had something to say but wasn't sure how to say it. When they reached her trailer behind the nursing home, he cut off the engine and cleared his throat.

"Kaylyn, I've worked with King for a long time,

ever since he and I were both just hourly laborers. So I think I know him just about as well as anybody. I can't guess what happened to tear you two apart, but I think you ought to know that he isn't a man to give up. He believes that when a man wants a thing, he just keeps working until he finds a way to get it. And he wants you."

"And I want him, Mac. But I don't know if I can have him and my own self-respect. I've always believed that if a thing is right, it'll work out. But not this time. Faith may move a mountain, or in this case *not* move a rock, and faith may keep the springs open. But there're going to be walls around them both that faith won't penetrate. No amount of believing is going to make the walls disappear."

"King tried," Mac said softly. "Give him a chance."

"I don't know, Mac," she said sadly. "I just don't know what to do. I have to work it out in my own mind."

For the next few weeks Kaylyn went through the motions of her normal routine. The residents of the Pretty Springs Nursing Home quickly learned not to mention either King Vandergriff or the springs. The bright yellow school buses that announced summer's end soon began their rounds of the neighborhood. The leaves started to streak with yellow and red. A heat wave tested tempers and the air-conditioning units as if it were pointing an I-told-you-so finger at Kaylyn's failed purpose.

The days seemed endless, and the sad, sympathetic glances of her patients turned Kaylyn into a walking zombie. What the hell was she going to do?

she kept asking herself. Minnie, Luther, even Harold needed her. But she had nothing to give. She was distracted and empty. Loving King Vandergriff had ended her life. She was alone. One day after the other she got up, performed her job, then went to bed to toss and turn without sleep.

Now it was mid-morning and she was in her office. Minnie and Luther were nowhere to be found. Everybody had just seen them, but nobody seemed to know where they were at the moment. Kaylyn leaned forward, resting her head on her arms.

King. He was all she could think of. He had tried to help her. They *had* saved the springs and the rock. Wasn't that enough? Couldn't she forgive him for what he couldn't control? She'd always known how to give love to those who needed it. Their giving love in return had been her lifeblood. Now that wasn't enough. Loving King had been more than a physical act. It had been a joining of their spirits, their very souls meshing into one being. Now she was only half a person.

Damn him! He'd taken her heart, her soul, and her faith. Somehow she had to get them back. But sitting here in her office feeling sorry for herself wasn't going to solve anything. She'd found that out already. The only answer for her was to go to King. There had to be a way. But if there wasn't, then she faced the harsh truth that she could no longer function without the man.

Kaylyn Smith and King Vandergriff had been inextricably bound together from that first moment on the rock. Magic? Fate? She didn't know, and she made no attempt to analyze it any longer. From the moment he'd climbed on top of Lizard Rock there had been an aura about them, an aura of love. She'd left part of herself at that rock. Now she was going back for it—and for King Vandergriff. She climbed into one of the nursing-home cars and cranked the engine.

A warm rush of happiness swept over her. She loved the man—Stetson, coordinated underwear, alligator boots, and all. She would find a way. She *had* found a way, she realized suddenly as she drove recklessly down the highway. And she knew as she turned into the drive and caught sight of the Lizard that she'd felt the return of her faith.

She brought the car to a screeching halt beside the great rock and took a deep breath, trying to marshal her thoughts. Somehow, some way, they'd find the answer. Then she heard them, the voices, King's deep tone and the woman's trilling laughter. There was a splashing sound. King and a woman—in the springs.

"Don't worry," King was saying. "This is going to be wonderful. Just relax and let me show you."

"You'd better not drop me," the woman answered, "I don't like the idea of the world knowing that this is how I met my end."

It was definitely King and a woman. He was turning her wonderful healing springs into a bordello. Then she heard another male voice. "Perfect, King." Damn, they were having an orgy.

Kaylyn's first thought was escape. She had even reached for the key in the ignition when a powerful sense of well-being washed over her. She sat for a long moment feeling the harsh emotions subside. Pretty Springs, her springs, King's springs. How could she have lost sight of the real issue?

The springs belonged to King now, but they'd been her refuge since the first time she'd heard about them. King's being there with someone else didn't change her plan. She'd come there to tell King that she was in love with him. If it took interrupting an assignation to do it, then so be it. She got out of the car and stood by the Lizard, gathering her courage.

King didn't believe in the healing power of the springs, but he'd learn. She'd teach him. He'd learn that their waters healed the body and that the quiet sense of well-being that surrounded the rocks and springs reached the mind—if one were willing to open oneself up to the mysterious powers of nature.

Strange, she thought, that she'd never seen that before. The Indians had come there and held ceremonies on the rock, asking for the gods to touch them. They'd shared their deepest sorrows and greatest joys with this place, and somehow those intense emotions had become a part of the rocks for all eternity. After the Indians the settlers had come and built a town and stayed. The spring waters had been bottled and sent out worldwide. Still, in the end, belief in their healing powers had gone out of vogue and they'd sunk into obscurity.

Now King had come and he and she had fallen in love. Through their love the springs would live on. Kaylyn reached out and touched the Lizard. She felt his surface grow warm beneath her hand and knew she had learned an important truth. Perhaps the real truth only made itself known to a few, but she was one of the chosen. She hadn't understood before. It was love that had made it possible. And King was chosen, too, only he didn't know it yet.

Filled with a growing sense of joy, she rounded the rock to confront King and his party and froze.

Standing waist-high in the clear water was King Vandergriff. He was holding Minnie Rakestraw while Sandi Arnold manipulated Minnie's thin legs. On the other side of the rocks were Tom Brolin, snapping pictures with a frenzy, and Luther Peavey, who was directing the entire operation.

"King?" Kaylyn said in astonishment.

"What'd I tell you?" Luther asked disgustedly. "I knew we wouldn't get away with this."

"What are you doing?" Kaylyn asked, then realized what a dumb thing she'd said.

"We're taking pictures," Sandi explained with a broad grin on her face.

"For King's publicity campaign," Tom added.

"It was to be a surprise," Minnie said, sounding peeved. "They insisted I put on a bathing suit and be in the picture—me, who's never worn a bathing suit in all my eighty-five years."

"I think we have enough, Minnie," Sandi said. "Luther, get her a towel." Sandi motioned to King, who was standing like a frozen statue in the water. Sandi shook her head, transferred Minnie's thin arms from King's neck to her own, and walked over to the edge of the pool.

Tom reached down and easily lifted Minnie from the water, then wrapped her in a thick towel.

"Which one of those old fools at the home told you where we were, Katie?" Luther asked.

"Nobody."

"See there, I told you they could keep a secret," Sandi said. "Well, Tom, if you think we have enough photographs, we'd better get Minnie and Luther back."

Kaylyn heard the others talking quietly as they

prepared to leave. But all she saw was King standing in the sunlight. His hair was wet and plastered to his head, as she'd seen so many times when they'd played in the water. He looked like the iron-faced savage she'd thought him to be the first time she'd seen him. Yet there was a new uncertainty in his face. He didn't speak.

"Nobody told me you were here," she repeated. "I came to see King." But she spoke to the rocks and the air. The others were gone.

"I've been waiting for you, Kaylyn," King said. "I wanted you to come, but I didn't want to force you until you'd made up your mind. Let me explain."

"No—not yet. I need to tell you. I'm here, King, because I love you." She untied the straps of her sundress, and let it slide down her body. "In the past few weeks I've thought about us constantly. You made me look at myself. I expected you to take my belief in the springs on faith, yet I wasn't willing to have faith in you. I was wrong. I never want to lose what we have. You're what I want, now and forever."

King was mesmerized. Beneath her dress she was wearing the same string bikini she had worn that first day. Like the old-world priestess he'd thought her to be, she stood beside the springs, ready to recite incantations to the gods. But the person on whom she was bestowing all her energy was himself. His words froze in his throat, and he could only lift his arms, opening himself to her with great joy.

"Be careful with your wishes, Kaylyn. Be very sure. I think you may get what you want."

Then she was in the water beside him. He could feel her in his arms before she even touched him.

His heart nearly burst when he saw the certainty in her eyes.

"King . . ." Her voice was trembling, not from fear but from emotion. "I came here to tell you that I love you, more than I'd ever thought I could love anybody. And even if you can only love me a little in return, my soul will have been healed."

Her mouth captured his in a kiss so sweet that the springs seemed to sing a special trill to celebrate the joy of their touch. As she felt the overwhelming sense of love intensify, her kiss deepened into a new kind of commitment of faith and forever.

King wanted to tell her that she had healed his soul as well, that she had filled the painful void in his life that he'd never before acknowledged to a living being. He wanted to say that she was the essence of the good that allowed man to love, and that he'd never, ever, let her go. But he only kissed her back, clinging to her with such force that his breath never seemed to reach his lungs.

All around them the springs gurgled and sang and caressed their burning skin.

She was barely conscious of being lifted from the water and laid on the grass beside the pool. She was lost to everything but the touch and feel of the golden man poised over her.

"You're so very beautiful, Katie, my love," he whispered hoarsely as he removed her bikini, his gaze traveling slowly and lovingly over her. His hands slid down her arm to her waist, then up across her ribs to her breast. The nipple peaked and trembled beneath his touch, and she waited, longing for the sweet tugging motion of his lips.

As he drew one nipple into his mouth she moaned

and gave herself over to the helpless need that burst out of control. She couldn't be still. She was burning with fire as she strained upward, aching for him to enter her, to join them together. She whispered his name over and over. "King, King, King, please . . ."

He moved over her body, and she parted her legs, eagerly opening herself to him. He drew back and looked down at her with great love and joy in his face. "My daring Kaylyn, my most darling Katie." He entered her, and time and place and worldly things fell away as they moved together in a ritual more intense than their bodies had ever known.

There was an energy, a loving that churned and intensified, separating them into millions of tiny particles of whirling fire before drawing them back together again. Like novas, their release was the explosive heat of nature, and they knew that they'd been fused forever.

At last King fell across Kaylyn, weak and shaken. "Are you all right?" He pushed himself up in alarm. She was so still. "Kaylyn?"

"I'm sorry," she whispered. "I'm skinny-dipping in silver lava. I can't possibly talk to a mere mortal. I have a god for a lover, and he's just taken me to the ends of the universe."

Her eyes were closed, her face was flushed, and there was the most wonderful peace about her smile. He'd been right to run the risks he'd run, he thought. They had been meant for each other from the first. His heart swelled as he contemplated the joy she'd feel when she learned what was going to happen. He bent down and kissed her, this woman who'd come to him despite believing that her springs had been lost to her patients. She loved him even after she thought he was going to destroy a thing she believed in.

Only the sound of construction behind the rocks kept him from making love to her again. He was ready. He felt the tenuous movement beneath him that announced her body stirring in response.

"Kaylyn, darling, I think we should move to our trailer. The rocks have shielded us from the workers so far, but you can never be sure when one of them might decide to cool off."

"Any man who puts his foot inside this circle will be hung at dawn," she said solemnly. "It is ordained. Nobody enters the sacred grounds without permission, except the king and his woman. However," she admitted, "the sacred grounds are becoming distinctly uncomfortable to the king's woman's backside."

"To the trailer," King said. He rose and pulled Kaylyn to her feet, then wrapped a towel around his nude body and held out his robe for her.

"A blue robe? Are you going soft on me?" She slipped into the robe and leaned back against him as his arms slid around her waist. He carefully folded one side of the robe over the other and pulled the belt tight.

"Not on your life, darling." He tightened his arms around her. "Does this feel soft?" He wasn't referring to the robe, and his reference point was anything but soft.

They managed to reach the trailer and get inside without being observed by any of his crew.

"Oh, King, it's beautiful."

The red-and-black decor had been completely replaced by soft blues and greens. The furniture consisted of puffy pillows and cushions spread over low-slung frames. The black and chrome was completely gone. The kitchen was now a creamy white to match the pale green cabinets and carpet.

"It's for you, Kaylyn. Blue for your eyes, green for the peaceful feelings you bring to this place. All for you. I want you to feel what I've learned about you and the springs." He turned her in his arms and looked directly into her eyes. "Loving you has changed my life."

"Oh, King, loving you has made my life different too. And I don't know how to handle the changes. I'm not like you. I've always been involved with other people. That was easier. It hurt, but it still wasn't me hurting for me. You've changed all that, and I feel as if I'm standing in sand that shifts every time I take a step."

"Let me show you the rest, my sweet love." He pushed the robe from her shoulders and lifted her into his arms. Somewhere between the tiny living room and the hall, his towel fell unnoticed to the floor.

"I started to get a smaller bed, but I didn't." He laid her on the pale blue down comforter and stepped back, gazing down at her with such love that she felt her entire being respond.

"You'd better not," she said breathlessly. "I'm a pretty big girl, and we're going to need every inch of this wonderful bed. That is, if you plan to join me here." She squirmed, twisting her legs from one side to the other. "What are you waiting for?"

"I want you to hear this." He knelt beside her, then leaned over her to the wall at the head of the bed. She totally missed his attention to a little box as she reached out eagerly to fondle him.

"Oh, King." She kissed his flat, hard rib cage and ran her tongue across his upper body. He shuddered and gasped, and then she heard the sweet sound.

"The springs. Oh, King."

The lilting melody of the springs filled the trailer as the water rushed forward and dropped gently, then fell in a crash of sound over the rocks and into the pool below.

"You've taped the springs, King. How lovely."

"Not nearly as lovely as you, my Katie. I've lain here night after night listening to the water, waiting for you to come to me so that I could show you how much I want you."

"Then show me, King. Show me."

"So now," Kaylyn said, "tell me about those pictures Tom was taking."

They were sitting cross-legged on the bed, feeding each other peach ice cream from a mixing bowl King was holding between his legs.

"Just a minute. You've got peaches on your chin." He leaned forward and caught the droplet of cream with his tongue. It seemed only natural to him then to slide upward and kiss her lips, sticky with the taste of peaches.

She pulled back. "King Vandergriff, at the rate we're going, the ice cream is going to melt. And I'm going to turn into some demented maniac if you don't tell me what you were doing."

"All right. You stay right here and let me put the ice cream in the freezer. Then we'll do some serious talking."

She smiled as she watched him walk down the hall. He was a spectacular man, she thought, every bronze-colored inch of his body. And there wasn't much of that body that she hadn't become intimately acquainted with.

When he returned and she caught sight of the expression on his face, she wasn't at all sure that what he had in mind was talking. It wasn't. But she had to admit that it was definitely serious.

The late-afternoon sun slipped over the rocks, throwing the trailer into the shadows. Kaylyn stirred and opened her eyes. King was leaning over her, studying her with such a look of love in his eyes that she never wanted to move.

"Talk time," he said. "Okay?"

"Yes."

"I did it, Katie, darlin'. Or rather, Joker did."

"Joker? What did he do?"

"He kept on working on our idea about the sports medicine center."

"He did?" She was having trouble focusing on King's words. His face was so good and kind, so very different from the stern man on the rock that first day, so different from the happy-go-lucky lover at the picnic. He was wonderful. Instinctively she wiggled closer.

"No, be still and stay away until I tell you."

"Oh, all right. Tell. What did your brother do?"

"Well, I told you we got the investors to agree to save the springs and the rock. But advancing more funds to convert the clubhouse into a serious rehabilitation center and spa was more than they'd do. So Joker and Diamond approached various players, baseball, basketball, football, and hockey players, who then went to their unions. That's what did it."

"Did what? If you don't get on with this, King Vandergriff, your royal family is going to have one less member."

"Well, let's just say that the Pretty Springs Sports Medicine and Therapeutic Center is now a part of the Golf and Tennis Club. We're going to have steam baths, heated pools, exercise and weight rooms, all open three days a week to outsiders who need these treatments. What do you think about that?"

Kaylyn was stunned, totally and completely stunned. For the first time in her adult life she was speechless. She lifted her head, making no attempt to hide the tears of joy that ran down her cheeks.

"You did this? For me?"

"No, my darling Kaylyn. We did this for us, our children, all the people who've come before, and all those who will come after." He caught her hand and brought it to his lips. "It was fate, darlin', our destiny."

Through the window Kaylyn caught sight of the Lizard, basking peacefully in the sunlight. A ripple of wind caught the limb of a nearby tree and threw a shadow across the face of the great stone creature. And for just a moment Kaylyn could have sworn he winked.

"You're right, King," she said, and turned her attention to the lips that had wandered up her wrist, her upper arm, and were now ascending with great determination toward her lips. It was "destiny."

Epilogue

"Good evening, ladies and gentlemen. This is Iris Raines, TV Nine, with a special report. Tonight we have a different kind of Christmas story, a story about two people on opposing sides of an issue who came together for the common good. Several months ago I was alerted to a protest being staged by a local woman to save a mineral springs dating back to the time of the Cherokee Indians. The springs were reported to have healing powers. . . ."

Iris went on to recap the story, beginning with the showdown at Lizard Rock and ending with the saving of the springs, and the subsequent wedding of the two people who had met, shared a common goal, and fallen in love.

The camera coverage switched from the springs to the wedding party posing on the front porch of the nursing home.

"Tonight's wedding was very special," Iris went on. "The Pretty Springs Nursing Home chapel was decorated with red poinsettia, green pine boughs, and Christmas candles. Every resident who could be made mobile was in attendance, along with the Pretty Springs city council, the members of the local Humane Society, and a group of very special men in the community who call themselves the Soupies. But that," Iris said with a warm smile, "is another story.

"As you can see, the crowd overflowed the small chapel and spilled out the hallway and into the yard, where a large group of townspeople have gathered to give their best wishes to the happy couple."

Iris identified Tom Brolin, editor of the *Pretty Springs Gazette*, who gave the bride away; Joker Vandergriff, a red-haired giant of a man with a bushy beard and mustache, the groom's younger brother; followed by Jack Vandergriff, the taller, dark-haired brother; and Mac Webster, foreman of the construction project. Beside the bride were Sandi Arnold, the maid of honor, and Diamond Vandergriff, sister of the groom.

But all eyes were on the couple in the center. Like exquisitely designed dolls, the striking blond couple stood, arms linked, gazing at each other in complete adoration. Her old-fashioned antique satin dress was beautiful, with lace trim and a long train. The groom's black tux was perfectly tailored to fit the magnificent body of the hawk-faced man.

Iris stepped into the crowd and held out her microphone. "Well, you two, you did it. You saved the springs and the rock. What do you plan to do for an encore?"

King tore his gaze from Kaylyn's face and faced the camera. "I haven't the wildest idea. But when you're married to a woman of the people, you never can tell."

"That's true," Kaylyn added shyly. "And when you're dealing with a self-made man, fate sometimes takes a hand. You just have to accept your destiny. Right now we need to cut a cake and drink our punch. We have a new baby back at the springs that we need to check on."

"What do you say we follow Matilda's lead?" King whispered suggestively in Kaylyn's ear as his hand innocently caressed the breast hidden by her flowers. "Quick!"

Kaylyn nodded, repositioned her huge bridal bouquet in front of them, and innocently slipped her hand into King's pocket.

King gasped, turned toward his bride, and pulled her into his arms. His kiss was urgent and passionate, allowing his great joy to be recorded for the world to see.

Iris gulped visibly and let the mike slip sideways in her hand. Inadvertently it picked up the conversation of an elderly man leaning over a woman in a wheelchair.

"Well, what'd you draw, Luther?" the woman asked.

"I've got a boy, in October. Pays twenty-five dollars. What about you?"

"Me?" The woman beamed. "Ha! I hit the jackpot. I've got twins in September for fifty big ones."

The television director quickly cut back to the springs. The picture of the Lizard glistened in the bright December moonlight. The camera angle gave an entirely different look to the great stone creature. This time his long snout seemed to curve upward, giving every suggestion of a satisfied smile.

THE EDITOR'S CORNER

Next month's LOVESWEPTs are sure to keep you warm as the first crisp winds of autumn nip the air! Rarely do our six books for the month have a common theme, but it just so happens our October group of LOVESWEPTs all deal with characters who must come to terms with their pasts in order to learn to love from the heart again.

In **RENEGADE,** LOVESWEPT #282, Judy Gill reunites a pair of lovers who have so many reasons for staying together, but who are pulled apart by old hurts. (Both have emotional scars that haven't yet healed.) When Jacqueline Train and Renny Knight struck a deal two years earlier, neither one expected their love to flourish in a marriage that had been purely a practical arrangement. And when Renny returns to claim her, Jacqueline is filled with panic . . . and sudden hope. But with tenderness, compassion, and overwhelming love Renny teaches her that the magic they'd created before was only a prelude to their real and enduring happiness.

LOVESWEPT #283, **ON WINGS OF FLAME,** is Gail Douglas's first published romance and one that is sure to establish her as a winner in the genre. When Jed Brannen offers Kelly Flynn the job of immortalizing his uncle's beloved pet in stained glass, she knows it's just a ploy on Jed's part. He's desperate to rekindle the romance that he'd walked away from years before. He'd been her Indiana Jones, roaming the globe in search of danger, and she'd almost managed to banish the memory of his tender caresses—until he returns in search of the only woman he's ever loved. Kelly's wounded pride makes her hold back from forgiving him, but every time she runs from him, she stumbles and falls . . . right into his arms.

Fayrene Preston brings you a jewel of a book in **EMERALD SUNSHINE,** LOVESWEPT #284. Too dazzled by the bright blue Dallas sky to keep her mind on the road, heroine Kathy Broderick rides her bike smack into Paul Garth's sleek limousine! The condition of her mangled bike isn't nearly as important to Kathy, however, as the condition of her heart when Paul offers her his help—

(continued)

and then his love. But resisting this man and the passionate hunger she feels for him, she finds, is as futile as pedaling backward. Paul has a few dark secrets he doesn't know how to share with Kathy. But as in all her romances, Fayrene brings these two troubled people together in a joyous union that won't fail to touch your soul.

TUCKER BOONE, LOVESWEPT #285, is Joan Elliott Pickart at her best! Alison Murdock has her work cut out for her as a lawyer who finds delivering Tucker's inheritance—an English butler—no small task. Swearing he's no gentleman, Tucker decides to uncover Alison's playful side—a side of herself she'd buried long ago under ambition and determination. Alison almost doesn't stop to consider what rugged, handsome Tucker Boone is doing to her orderly life, until talk of the future makes her remember the past—and her vow to rise to the top of her profession. Luckily Tucker convinces her that reaching new heights in his arms is the most important goal of all!

Kay Hooper has written the romance you've all been waiting for! In **SHADES OF GRAY,** LOVESWEPT #286, Kay tells the love story of the charismatic island ruler, Andres Sereno, first introduced in **RAFFERTY'S WIFE** last November. Sara Marsh finds that loving the man who'd abducted her to keep her safe from his enemies is something as elemental to her as breathing. But when Sara sees the violent side of Andres, she can't reconcile it with the sensitive, exquisitely passionate man she knows him to be. Andres realizes that loving Sara fuels the goodness in him, fills him with urgent need. And Sara can't control the force of her love for Andres any more than he can stop himself from doing what must be done to save his island of Kadeira. Suddenly she learns that nothing appears black and white to her anymore. She can see only shades of gray . . . and all the hues of love.

Following her debut as a LOVESWEPT author with her book **DIVINE DESIGN,** published in June, Mary Kay McComas is back on the scene with her second book for us, **OBSESSION,** LOVESWEPT #287. A powerful tale of a woman overcoming the injustices of her past with the help of a man who knows her more intimately than

(continued)

any other person on earth—before he even meets her—Mary Kay weaves an emotional web of romance and desire. Esther Brite is known to the world as a famous songwriter, one half of a the husband and wife team that brought music into the lives of millions. But when her husband and son are killed in a car accident, Esther returns to her hometown, where she'd once been shunned, searching for answers to questions she isn't sure she wants to ask. Doctor Dan Jacobey has reasons of his own for seeking sanctuary in the town of Bellewood—the one place where he could feel close to the woman he'd become obsessed with—Esther Brite. Esther and Dan discover that together they are not afraid to face the demons of the past and promise each other a beautiful tomorrow.

I think you're going to savor and enjoy each of the books next month as if you were feasting on a gourmet six-course meal!

Bon appetite!

Carolyn Nichols

Carolyn Nichols
Editor

LOVESWEPT
Bantam Books
666 Fifth Avenue
New York, NY 10103

THE HOMETOWN HUNK CONTEST

FOR EVERY WOMAN WHO HAS EVER SAID—
"I know a man who looks
just like the hero of this book"
—HAVE WE GOT A CONTEST FOR YOU!

To help celebrate our fifth year of publishing LOVESWEPT we are having a fabulous, fun-filled event called THE HOMETOWN HUNK contest. We are going to reissue six classic early titles by six of your favorite authors.

DARLING OBSTACLES by Barbara Boswell
IN A CLASS BY ITSELF by Sandra Brown
C.J.'S FATE by Kay Hooper
THE LADY AND THE UNICORN by Iris Johansen
CHARADE by Joan Elliott Pickart
FOR THE LOVE OF SAMI by Fayrene Preston

Here, as in the backs of all July, August, and September 1988 LOVESWEPTS you will find "cover notes" just like the ones we prepare at Bantam as the background for our art director to create our covers. These notes will describe the hero and heroine, give a teaser on the plot, and suggest a scene for the cover. Your part in the contest will be to see if a great looking local man—or men, if your hometown is so blessed—fits our description of one of the heroes of the six books we will reissue.

THE HOMETOWN HUNK who is selected (one for each of the six titles) will be flown to New York via United Airlines and will stay at the Loews Summit Hotel—the ideal hotel for business or pleasure in midtown Manhattan—for two nights. All travel arrangements made by Reliable Travel International, Incorporated. He will be the model for the new cover of the book which will be released in mid-1989. The six people who send in the winning photos of their HOMETOWN HUNK will receive a pre-selected assortment of LOVESWEPT books free for one year. Please see the Official Rules above the Official Entry Form for full details and restrictions.

We can't wait to start judging those pictures! Oh, and you must let the man you've chosen know that you're entering him in the contest. After all, if he wins he'll have to come to New York.

Have fun. Here's your chance to get the cover-lover of your dreams!

Carolyn Nichols
Editor
LOVESWEPT
Bantam Books
666 Fifth Avenue
New York, NY 10102–0023

THE HOMETOWN HUNK CONTEST

DARLING OBSTACLES

(Originally Published as LOVESWEPT #95)

By Barbara Boswell

COVER NOTES

The Characters:

Hero:
GREG WILDER's gorgeous body and "to-die-for" good looks haven't hurt him in the dating department, but when most women discover he's a widower with four kids, they head for the hills! Greg has the hard, muscular build of an athlete, and his light brown hair, which he wears neatly parted on the side, is streaked blond by the sun. Add to that his aquamarine blue eyes that sparkle when he laughs, and his sensual mouth and generous lower lip, and you're probably wondering what woman in her right mind wouldn't want Greg's strong, capable surgeon's hands working their magic on her—kids or no kids!

Personality Traits:
An acclaimed neurosurgeon, Greg Wilder is a celebrity of sorts in the planned community of Woodland, Maryland. Authoritative, debonair, self-confident, his reputation for engaging in one casual relationship after another almost overshadows his prowess as a doctor. In reality, Greg dates more out of necessity than anything else, since he has to attend one social function after another. He considers most of the events boring and wishes he could spend more time with his children. But his profession is a difficult and demanding one—and being both father and mother to four kids isn't any less so. A thoughtful, generous, sometimes befuddled father, Greg tries to do it all. Cerebral, he uses his intellect and skill rather than physical strength to win his victories. However, he never expected to come up against one Mary Magdalene May!

Heroine:
MARY MAGDALENE MAY, called Maggie by her friends, is the thirty-two-year-old mother of three children. She has shoulder-length auburn hair, and green eyes that shout her Irish heritage. With high cheekbones and an upturned nose covered with a smattering of freckles, Maggie thinks of herself more as the girl-next-door type. Certainly, she believes, she could never be one of Greg Wilder's beautiful escorts.

Setting: The small town of Woodland, Maryland

The Story:
Surgeon Greg Wilder wanted to court the feisty and beautiful widow who'd been caring for his four kids, but she just wouldn't let him past her doorstep! Sure that his interest was only casual, and that he preferred more sophisticated women, Maggie May vowed to keep Greg at arm's length. But he wouldn't take no for an answer. And once he'd crashed through her defenses and pulled her into his arms, he was tireless—and reckless—in his campaign to win her over. Maggie had found it tough enough to resist one determined doctor; now he threatened to call in his kids and hers as reinforcements—seven rowdy snags to romance!

Cover scene:
As if romancing Maggie weren't hard enough, Greg can't seem to find time to spend with her without their children around. Stealing a private moment on the stairs in Maggie's house, Greg and Maggie embrace. She is standing one step above him, but she still has to look up at him to see into his eyes. Greg's hands are on her hips, and her hands are resting on his shoulders. Maggie is wearing a very sheer, short pink nightgown, and Greg has on wheat-colored jeans and a navy and yellow striped rugby shirt. Do they have time to kiss?

THE HOMETOWN HUNK CONTEST

IN A CLASS BY ITSELF

(Originally Published as LOVESWEPT #66)

By Sandra Brown

COVER NOTES

The Characters:

Hero:
LOGAN WEBSTER would have no trouble posing for a Scandinavian travel poster. His wheat-colored hair always seems to be tousled, defying attempts to control it, and falls across his wide forehead. Thick eyebrows one shade darker than his hair accentuate his crystal blue eyes. He has a slender nose that flairs slightly over a mouth that testifies to both sensitivity and strength. The faint lines around his eyes and alongside his mouth give the impression that reaching the ripe age of 30 wasn't all fun and games for him. Logan's square, determined jaw is punctuated by a vertical cleft. His broad shoulders and narrow waist add to his tall, lean appearance.

Personality traits:
Logan Webster has had to scrape and save and fight for everything he's gotten. Born into a poor farm family, he was driven to succeed and overcome his "wrong side of the tracks" image. His businesses include cattle, real estate, and natural gas. Now a pillar of the community, Logan's life has been a true rags-to-riches story. Only Sandra Brown's own words can describe why he is masculinity epitomized: "Logan had 'the walk,' that saddle-tramp saunter that was inherent to native Texan men, passed down through generations of cowboys. It was, without even trying to be, sexy. The unconscious roll of the hips, the slow strut, the flexed knees, the slouching stance, the deceptive laziness that hid a latent aggressiveness." Wow! And not only does he have "the walk," but he's fun

and generous and kind. Even with his wealth, he feels at home living in his small hometown with simple, hard-working, middle-class, backbone-of-America folks. A born leader, people automatically gravitate toward him.

Heroine:
DANI QUINN is a sophisticated twenty-eight-year-old woman. Dainty, her body compact, she is utterly feminine. Dani's pale, lustrous hair is moonlight and honey spun together, and because it is very straight, she usually wears it in a chignon. With golden eyes to match her golden hair, Dani is the one woman Logan hasn't been able to get off his mind for the ten years they've been apart.

Setting: Primarily on Logan's ranch in East Texas.

The Story:
Ten years had passed since Dani Quinn had graduated from high school in the small Texas town, ten years since the night her elopement with Logan Webster had ended in disaster. Now Dani approached her tenth reunion with uncertainty. Logan would be there . . . Logan, the only man who'd ever made her shiver with desire and need, but would she have the courage to face the fury in his eyes? She couldn't defend herself against his anger and hurt—to do so would demand she reveal the secret sorrow she shared with no one. Logan's touch had made her his so long ago. Could he reach past the pain to make her his for all time?

Cover Scene:
It's sunset, and Logan and Dani are standing beside the swimming pool on his ranch, embracing. The pool is surrounded by semitropical plants and lush flower beds. In the distance, acres of rolling pasture land resembling a green lake undulate into dense, piney woods. Dani is wearing a strapless, peacock blue bikini and sandals with leather ties that wrap around her ankles. Her hair is straight and loose, falling to the middle of her back. Logan has on a light-colored pair of corduroy shorts and a short-sleeved designer knit shirt in a pale shade of yellow.

THE HOMETOWN HUNK CONTEST

C.J.'S FATE

(Originally Published as LOVESWEPT #32)

By Kay Hooper

COVER NOTES

The Characters:

Hero:
FATE WESTON easily could have walked straight off an Indian reservation. His raven black hair and strong, well-molded features testify to his heritage. But somewhere along the line genetics threw Fate a curve—his eyes are the deepest, darkest blue imaginable! Above those blue eyes are dark slanted eyebrows, and fanning out from those eyes are faint laugh lines—the only sign of the fact that he's thirty-four years old. Tall, Fate moves with easy, loose-limbed grace. Although he isn't an athlete, Fate takes very good care of himself, and it shows in his strong physique. Striking at first glance and fascinating with each succeeding glance, the serious expressions on his face make him look older than his years, but with one smile he looks boyish again.

Personality traits:
Fate possesses a keen sense of humor. His heavy-lidded, intelligent eyes are capable of concealment, but there is a shrewdness in them that reveals the man hadn't needed college or a law degree to be considered intelligent. The set of his head tells you that he is proud—perhaps even a bit arrogant. He is attractive and perfectly well aware of that fact. Unconventional, paradoxical, tender, silly, lusty, gentle, comical, serious, absurd, and endearing are all words that come to mind when you think of Fate. He is not ashamed to be everything a man can be. A defense attorney by profession, one can detect a bit of frustrated actor in his character. More than anything else, though, it's the

impression of humor about him—reinforced by the elusive dimple in his cheek—that makes Fate Weston a scrumptious hero!

Heroine:
C.J. ADAMS is a twenty-six-year-old research librarian. Unaware of her own attractiveness, C.J. tends to play down her pixylike figure and tawny gold eyes. But once she meets Fate, she no longer feels that her short, burnished copper curls and the sprinkling of freckles on her nose make her unappealing. He brings out the vixen in her, and changes the smart, bookish woman who professed to have no interest in men into the beautiful, sexy woman she really was all along. Now, if only he could get her to tell him what C.J. stands for!

Setting: Ski lodge in Aspen, Colorado

The Story:
C.J. Adams had been teased enough about her seeming lack of interest in the opposite sex. On a ski trip with her five best friends, she impulsively embraced a handsome stranger, pretending they were secret lovers—and the delighted lawyer who joined in her impetuous charade seized the moment to deepen the kiss. Astonished at his reaction, C.J. tried to nip their romance in the bud—but found herself nipping at his neck instead! She had met her match in a man who could answer her witty remarks with clever ripostes of his own, and a lover whose caresses aroused in her a passionate need she'd never suspected that she could feel. Had destiny somehow tossed them together?

Cover Scene:
C.J. and Fate virtually have the ski slopes to themselves early one morning, and they take advantage of it! Frolicking in a snow drift, Fate is covering C.J. with snow—and kisses! They are flushed from the cold weather and from the excitement of being in love. C.J. is wearing a sky-blue one-piece, tight-fitting ski outfit that zips down the front Fate is wearing a navy blue parka and matching ski pants

THE HOMETOWN HUNK CONTEST

THE LADY AND THE UNICORN

(Originally Published as LOVESWEPT #29)

By Iris Johansen

COVER NOTES

The Characters:

Hero:
Not classically handsome, RAFE SANTINE's blunt, craggy features reinforce the quality of overpowering virility about him. He has wide, Slavic cheekbones and a bold, thrusting chin, which give the impression of strength and authority. Thick black eyebrows are set over piercing dark eyes. He wears his heavy, dark hair long. His large frame measures in at almost six feet four inches, and it's hard to believe that a man with such brawny shoulders and strong thighs could exhibit the pantherlike grace which characterizes Rafe's movements. Rafe Santine is definitely a man to be reckoned with, and heroine Janna Cannon does just that!

Personality traits:
Our hero is a man who radiates an aura of power and danger, and women find him intriguing and irresistible. Rafe Santine is a self-made billionaire at the age of thirty-eight. Almost entirely self-educated, he left school at sixteen to work on his first construction job, and by the time he was twenty-three, he owned the company. From there he branched out into real estate, computers, and oil. Rafe reportedly changes mistresses as often as he changes shirts. His reputation for ruthless brilliance has been earned over years of fighting to the top of the economic ladder from the slums of New York. His gruff manner and hard personality hide the tender, vulnerable side of him. Rafe also possesses an insatiable thirst for knowledge that is a passion with him. Oddly enough, he has a wry sense of

humor that surfaces unexpectedly from time to time. And, though cynical to the extreme, he never lets his natural skepticism interfere with his innate sense of justice.

Heroine:
JANNA CANNON, a game warden for a small wildlife preserve, is a very dedicated lady. She is tall at five feet nine inches and carries herself in a stately way. Her long hair is dark brown and is usually twisted into a single thick braid in back. Of course, Rafe never lets her keep her hair braided when they make love! Janna is one quarter Cherokee Indian by heritage, and she possesses the dark eyes and skin of her ancestors.

Setting: Rafe's estate in Carmel, California

The Story:
Janna Cannon scaled the high walls of Rafe Santine's private estate, afraid of nothing and determined to appeal to the powerful man who could save her beloved animal preserve. She bewitched his guard dogs, then cast a spell of enchantment over him as well. Janna's profound grace, her caring nature, made the tough and proud Rafe grow mercurial in her presence. She offered him a gift he'd never risked reaching out for before—but could he trust his own emotions enough to open himself to her love?

Cover Scene:
In the gazebo overlooking the rugged cliffs at the edge of the Pacific Ocean, Rafe and Janna share a passionate moment together. The gazebo is made of redwood and the interior is small and cozy. Scarlet cushions cover the benches, and matching scarlet curtains hang from the eaves, caught back by tasseled sashes to permit the sea breeze to whip through the enclosure. Rafe is wearing black suede pants and a charcoal gray crew-neck sweater. Janna is wearing a safari-style khaki shirt-and-slacks outfit and suede desert boots. They embrace against the breathtaking backdrop of wild, crashing, white-crested waves pounding the rocks and cliffs below.

THE HOMETOWN HUNK CONTEST

CHARADE

(Originally Published as LOVESWEPT #74)

By Joan Elliott Pickart

COVER NOTES

The Characters:

Hero:
The phrase tall, dark, and handsome was coined to describe TENNES WHITNEY. His coal black hair reaches past his collar in back, and his fathomless steel gray eyes are framed by the kind of thick, dark lashes that a woman would kill to have. Darkly tanned, Tennes has a straight nose and a square chin, with—you guessed it!—a Kirk Douglas cleft. Tennes oozes masculinity and virility. He's a handsome son-of-a-gun!

Personality traits:
A shrewd, ruthless business tycoon, Tennes is a man of strength and principle. He's perfected the art of buying floundering companies and turning them around financially, then selling them at a profit. He possesses a sixth sense about business—in short, he's a winner! But there are two sides to his personality. Always in cool command, Tennes, who fears no man or challenge, is rendered emotionally vulnerable when faced with his elderly aunt's illness. His deep devotion to the woman who raised him clearly casts him as a warm, compassionate guy—not at all like the tough-as-nails executive image he presents. Leave it to heroine Whitney Jordan to discover the real man behind the complicated enigma.

Heroine:
WHITNEY JORDAN's russet-colored hair floats past her shoulders in glorious waves. Her emerald green eyes, full breasts, and long, slender legs—not to mention her peaches-

and-cream complexion—make her eye-poppingly attractive. How can Tennes resist the twenty-six-year-old beauty? And how can Whitney consider becoming serious with him? If their romance flourishes, she may end up being Whitney Whitney!

Setting: Los Angeles, California

The Story:
One moment writer Whitney Jordan was strolling the aisles of McNeil's Department Store, plotting the untimely demise of a soap opera heartthrob; the next, she was nearly knocked over by a real-life stunner who implored her to be his fiancée! The ailing little gray-haired aunt who'd raised him had one final wish, he said—to see her dear nephew Tennes married to the wonderful girl he'd described in his letters . . . only that girl hadn't existed—until now! Tennes promised the masquerade would last only through lunch, but Whitney gave such an inspired performance that Aunt Olive refused to let her go. And what began as a playful romantic deception grew more breathlessly real by the minute. . . .

Cover Scene:
Whitney's living room is bright and cheerful. The gray carpeting and blue sofa with green and blue throw pillows gives the apartment a cool but welcoming appearance. Sitting on the sofa next to Tennes, Whitney is wearing a black crepe dress that is simply cut but stunning. It is cut low over her breasts and held at the shoulders by thin straps. The skirt falls to her knees in soft folds and the bodice is nipped in at the waist with a matching belt. She has on black high heels, but prefers not to wear any jewelry to spoil the simplicity of the dress. Tennes is dressed in a black suit with a white silk shirt and a deep red tie.

THE HOMETOWN HUNK CONTEST

FOR THE LOVE OF SAMI

(Originally Published as LOVESWEPT #34)

By Fayrene Preston

COVER NOTES

Hero:
DANIEL PARKER-ST. JAMES is every woman's dream come true. With glossy black hair and warm, reassuring blue eyes, he makes our heroine melt with just a glance. Daniel's lean face is chiseled into assertive planes. His lips are full and firmly sculptured, and his chin has the determined and arrogant thrust to it only a man who's sure of himself can carry off. Daniel has a lot in common with Clark Kent. Both wear glasses, and when Daniel removes them to make love to Sami, she thinks he really is Superman!

Personality traits:
Daniel Parker-St. James is one of the Twin Cities' most respected attorneys. He's always in the news, either in the society columns with his latest society lady, or on the front page with his headline cases. He's brilliant and takes on only the toughest cases—usually those that involve millions of dollars. Daniel has a reputation for being a deadly opponent in the courtroom. Because he's from a socially prominent family and is a Harvard graduate, it's expected that he'll run for the Senate one day. Distinguished-looking and always distinctively dressed—he's fastidious about his appearance—Daniel gives off an unassailable air of authority and absolute control.

Heroine:
SAMUELINA (SAMI) ADKINSON is secretly a wealthy heiress. No one would guess. She lives in a converted warehouse loft, dresses to suit no one but herself, and dabbles in the creative arts. Sami is twenty-six years old, with

long, honey-colored hair. She wears soft, wispy bangs and has very thick brown lashes framing her golden eyes. Of medium height, Sami has to look up to gaze into Daniel's deep blue eyes.

Setting: St. Paul, Minnesota

The Story:
Unpredictable heiress Sami Adkinson had endeared herself to the most surprising people—from the bag ladies in the park she protected . . . to the mobster who appointed himself her guardian . . . to her exasperated but loving friends. Then Sami was arrested while demonstrating to save baby seals, and it took powerful attorney Daniel Parker-St. James to bail her out. Daniel was smitten, soon cherishing Sami and protecting her from her night fears. Sami reveled in his love—and resisted it too. And holding on to Sami, Daniel discovered, was like trying to hug quicksilver. . . .

Cover Scene:
The interior of Daniel's house is very grand and supremely formal, the decor sophisticated, refined, and quietly tasteful, just like Daniel himself. Rich traditional fabrics cover plush oversized custom sofas and Regency wing chairs. Queen Anne furniture is mixed with Chippendale and is subtly complemented with Oriental accent pieces. In the library, floor-to-ceiling bookcases filled with rare books provide the backdrop for Sami and Daniel's embrace. Sami is wearing a gold satin sheath gown. The dress has a high neckline, but in back is cut provocatively to the waist. Her jewels are exquisite. The necklace is made up of clusters of flowers created by large, flawless diamonds. From every cluster a huge, perfectly matched teardrop emerald hangs. The earrings are composed of an even larger flower cluster, and an equally huge teardrop-shaped emerald hangs from each one. Daniel is wearing a classic, elegant tuxedo.

LOVESWEPT® HOMETOWN HUNK CONTEST

OFFICIAL RULES

IN A CLASS BY ITSELF by Sandra Brown
FOR THE LOVE OF SAMI by Fayrene Preston
C.J.'S FATE by Kay Hooper
THE LADY AND THE UNICORN by Iris Johansen
CHARADE by Joan Elliott Pickart
DARLING OBSTACLES by Barbara Boswell

1. NO PURCHASE NECESSARY. Enter the HOMETOWN HUNK contest by completing the Official Entry Form below and enclosing a sharp color full-length photograph (easy to see details, with the photo being no smaller than 2½" × 3½") of the man you think perfectly represents one of the heroes from the above-listed books which are described in the accompanying Loveswept cover notes. Please be sure to fill out the Official Entry Form completely, and also be sure to clearly print on the back of the man's photograph the man's name, address, city, state, zip code, telephone number, date of birth, your name, address, city, state, zip code, telephone number, your relationship, if any, to the man (e.g. wife, girlfriend) as well as the title of the Loveswept book for which you are entering the man. If you do not have an Official Entry Form, you can print all of the required information on a 3" × 5" card and attach it to the photograph with all the necessary information printed on the back of the photograph as well. YOUR HERO MUST SIGN BOTH THE BACK OF THE OFFICIAL ENTRY FORM (OR 3" × 5" CARD) AND THE PHOTOGRAPH TO SIGNIFY HIS CONSENT TO BEING ENTERED IN THE CONTEST. Completed entries should be sent to:

BANTAM BOOKS
HOMETOWN HUNK CONTEST
Department CN
666 Fifth Avenue
New York, New York 10102–0023

All photographs and entries become the property of Bantam Books and will not be returned under any circumstances.

2. Six men will be chosen by the Loveswept authors as a HOMETOWN HUNK (one HUNK per Loveswept title). By entering the contest, each winner and each person who enters a winner agrees to abide by Bantam Books' rules and to be subject to Bantam Books' eligibility requirements. Each winning HUNK and each person who enters a winner will be required to sign all papers deemed necessary by Bantam Books before receiving any prize. Each winning HUNK will be flown via **United Airlines** from his closest United Airlines-serviced city to New York City and will stay at the SUMMIT Hotel—the ideal hotel for business or pleasure in midtown Manhattan—for two nights. Winning HUNKS' meals and hotel transfers will be provided by Bantam Books. Travel and hotel arrangements are made by Reliable Travel International, Inc. and are subject to availability and to Bantam Books' date requirements. Each winning HUNK will pose with a female model at a photographer's studio for a photograph that will serve as the basis of a Loveswept front cover. Each winning HUNK will receive a $150.00 modeling fee. Each winning HUNK will be required to sign an Affidavit of Eligibility and Model's Release supplied by Bantam Books. (Approximate retail value of HOMETOWN HUNK'S PRIZE: $900.00). The six people who send in a winning HOMETOWN HUNK photograph that is used by Bantam will receive free for one year each, LOVESWEPT romance paperback books published by Bantam during that year. (Approximate retail value: $180.00.) Each person who submits a winning photograph

will also be required to sign an Affidavit of Eligibility and Promotional Release supplied by Bantam Books. All winning HUNKS' (as well as the people who submit the winning photographs) names, addresses, biographical data and likenesses may be used by Bantam Books for publicity and promotional purposes without any additional compensation. There will be no prize substitutions or cash equivalents made.

3. All completed entries must be received by Bantam Books no later than September 15, 1988. Bantam Books is not responsible for lost or misdirected entries. The finalists will be selected by Loveswept editors and the six winning HOMETOWN HUNKS will be selected by the six authors of the participating Loveswept books. Winners will be selected on the basis of how closely the judges believe they reflect the descriptions of the books' heroes. Winners will be notified on or about October 31, 1988. If there are insufficient entries or if in the judges' opinions, no entry is suitable or adequately reflects the descriptions of the hero(s) in the book(s), Bantam may decide not to award a prize for the applicable book(s) and may reissue the book(s) at its discretion.

4. The contest is open to residents of the U.S. and Canada, except the Province of Quebec, and is void where prohibited by law. All federal and local regulations apply. Employees of Reliable Travel International, Inc., United Airlines, the Summit Hotel, and the Bantam Doubleday Dell Publishing Group, Inc., their subsidiaries and affiliates, and their immediate families are ineligible to enter.

5. For an extra copy of the Official Rules, the Official Entry Form, and the accompanying Loveswept cover notes, send your request and a self-addressed stamped envelope (Vermont and Washington State residents need not affix postage) before August 20, 1988 to the address listed in Paragraph 1 above.

LOVESWEPT® HOMETOWN HUNK OFFICIAL ENTRY FORM

BANTAM BOOKS
HOMETOWN HUNK CONTEST
Dept. CN
666 Fifth Avenue
New York, New York 10102–0023

HOMETOWN HUNK CONTEST

YOUR NAME______________________________

YOUR ADDRESS______________________________

CITY______________ STATE______________ ZIP________

THE NAME OF THE LOVESWEPT BOOK FOR WHICH YOU ARE ENTERING THIS PHOTO

______________________by______________________

YOUR RELATIONSHIP TO YOUR HERO______________________

YOUR HERO'S NAME______________________________

YOUR HERO'S ADDRESS______________________________

CITY______________ STATE______________ ZIP________

YOUR HERO'S TELEPHONE #______________________

YOUR HERO'S DATE OF BIRTH______________________

YOUR HERO'S SIGNATURE CONSENTING TO HIS PHOTOGRAPH ENTRY

____